THE HORSESHOE TRILOGIES

Keeping Faith

Read all the books in the Horseshoe Trilogies:

Book #1: Keeping Faith

COMING SOON:
Book #2: Last Hope
Book #3: Sweet Charity

THE HORSESHOE TRILOGIES

Keeping Faith

by
Lucy Daniels

HYPERION
New York

Special thanks to Jennie Walters.
Thanks also to Richard Jones, M.R.C.V.S., for reviewing the
veterinary material contained in this book.

First published in England by Hodder Children's Books under the series title
Perfect Ponies.

Printed in the United States of America

First U.S. edition, 2002
3 5 7 9 10 8 6 4
This book is set in 12.5-point Life Roman.
ISBN 0-7868-1618-X (paperback ed.)
ISBN 0-7868-1960-X (hardcover ed.)
Visit www.volobooks.com

To Eva Melin—a perfect friend

THE HORSESHOE TRILOGIES

Keeping Faith

CHAPTER ONE

Josie Grace jumped down the last step from the bus to the pavement and stood there for a moment, hesitating.

"Come on, Josie!" said her friend Anna Marshall, following on behind and jostling her out of the way. "There's going to be a pileup if you don't move."

Anna's twin brother, Ben, was close on her heels, swinging a huge backpack stuffed full of schoolbooks and his soccer cleats. "Are you okay, Josie?" he asked quietly as the bus drove away. "You haven't said a word since we left school. Is anything wrong?"

"No, not really," Josie muttered. "It's just that— oh, it doesn't matter."

"Of course! How could I have forgotten?" Anna groaned, hitting herself on the forehead with the palm of her hand. "Oh, Josie, I'm sorry. Some friend I am! The local paper comes out today, doesn't it?"

"So what?" said Ben, looking puzzled. "Why's that such a big deal?"

"I'll explain in a minute," said his sister, hustling him off toward the village of Northgate, where they lived. "I'll come by and see you later," she called back to Josie. "Promise me you won't get depressed!"

"I promise," Josie said with a wave and an attempt at a smile.

Josie and Anna had met three years before when they were nine years old, and they had been best friends since that day. The twins' parents had separated, so Ben, Anna, and their mother had moved into a little terraced house in the village. Josie had been put in charge of looking after Anna on her first day as a new girl at school, and they had hit it off right away. The very next weekend, Ben and Anna turned up to help at the riding stables Josie's mother ran, and before long it had become their second home.

Josie watched as the Marshall twins made their

way down the road. Anna was talking like a chatterbox as usual, and Ben was bouncing a tennis ball, not paying her much attention. They both had the same olive skin and black hair, though Ben's was curly and Anna's was straight.

"It's not fair," Josie often grumbled as she dragged a brush through her own untidy auburn waves. "How come your hair always looks so perfect?"

"Well, how come you have blue eyes and I've got boring brown ones?" Anna would retort, and that always shut Josie up.

With a sigh, Josie swung her bag more comfortably over her shoulder and started walking in the opposite direction toward Grace's Riding Stables. Usually she couldn't wait to get back home from school, change into jeans and then rush outside to help her mother with the horses. Today, though, was different. There was something waiting for her at home she'd rather not see.

When she reached the driveway, she could hear her mother's encouraging voice floating across from the outdoor schooling ring. "That's it, Michael! Up, down, up, down, up, down. You know, I think you've got the hang of rising trot now!"

Well, you have been coming here for a year, Michael Lee, Josie thought grumpily to herself. She stopped for a second to lean on the gate and to watch. If you don't get the hang of it soon, you never will. She was in no mood to be kind to anyone, which was unlike her.

Returning her mother's wave, Josie continued walking past the duckpond and up a narrow path to School Farm, the low thatched cottage where the Graces lived. She stepped over a pair of riding boots on the porch and pushed open the heavy front door.

"Calm down, Basil," she said, as the family's mongrel terrier threw himself at her, wagging his tail and licking her hand enthusiastically. She gave him an absentminded pat and he followed her down a short hallway into the kitchen, his claws clicking on the wooden floorboards.

The newspaper was lying on the kitchen table. With her heart thumping, Josie dropped her schoolbag and began to turn the pages until she reached the classified ads. She scanned the columns quickly, hardly daring to look too closely, until her eyes came to rest on a short, boxed advertisement.

Josie let out another long sigh and read the advertisement once more before closing the paper. So there it was, in black and white. She still found it hard to believe that they really had to part with Faith, who had been around ever since Josie could remember. She first rode when she was three years old, and Faith was the first horse she'd ever ridden. The mare was always patient and calm, and Josie's confidence had grown from the first day she'd been placed on Faith's broad, comfortable back.

Josie went over to the big wooden dresser and picked up a framed photograph from one of the shelves. She smiled as she looked at herself. In the picture was a solemn little girl with curly reddish-brown hair, on top of a steady bay horse. She was clutching a handful of mane and holding on for dear life, her plump little legs stuck straight out on either side.

Suddenly the door swung open and Mary Grace came rushing into the kitchen. "Hello, sweetheart," she said, giving her daughter a hug. "What did you think of Michael today? He's coming along, isn't he?" And then she noticed the photo Josie was looking at, and her face became more serious. "Are you feeling all right?" she asked sympathetically.

"Would it make any difference if I wasn't?" Josie replied grumpily.

"Oh, don't be like that," her mother said, sighing heavily. She sat down at the table, glancing at the newspaper before pushing it quickly to one side. "I don't want to lose Faith any more than you do. She was my first horse here, remember? You know there's nothing we can do about it. The stables have got to close, and we've got to find new homes for all the horses. We've been over all this a hundred times—there's no alternative."

"Oh, why did Mrs. Wetherall have to die?" Josie groaned, pulling out a chair opposite her mother and slumping into it. "And why did her horrible nephew have to go and inherit everything?"

Mrs. Wetherall was the old lady who'd owned School Farm, the stables and the fields where the horses grazed. She'd lived on her own in a large house in the village, and had been happy for the Graces to rent the property from her very cheaply.

"I just want the place to be put to good use," she'd said.

But then, out of the blue, Mrs. Wetherall had had a stroke and died a few days later. After a couple of weeks of uncertainty, the Graces had received a letter from her nephew's lawyers. The letter told them that he was the new owner and that they had three months to find "other accommodations" and leave the house and the stables.

"Well, we always knew it couldn't go on forever," said Mrs. Grace. "We were leasing the house and stables from her at such a low rent. We just didn't expect it to end quite so suddenly. But it's not really fair to expect her nephew to continue the arrangement. He'll get five times the money if he sells the site to a developer."

"Are you *sure* we can't afford to buy it ourselves?" Josie asked desperately.

"On your father's salary?" answered her mother, smiling ruefully. "I'm afraid not, dear. Teachers don't get paid that much, and we only make enough out of the stables to cover our costs."

"Couldn't we find some other property to rent, though?" Josie asked, jumping up impatiently from her chair and pacing around the kitchen. "Then we could just move the horses there and continue as we are now."

"No, that's just not an option," her mother replied. "To start off with, we'd never find anywhere with such a low rent, and for so few horses. All the other stables around here are for fifteen or twenty horses at least. We couldn't possibly afford to expand so suddenly."

"We could if we got a bank loan," Josie said stubbornly, leaning against the dresser and folding her arms.

"But bank loans have to be paid back, Josie," said Mrs. Grace. "Oh, come on, sweetheart, we've talked all this over. You know what the plan is. Hope and Charity will stay with us for as long as possible, so we can continue using them for teaching. And we've started looking for Faith's new home now, so that we've got ample time to make sure she'll be really happy wherever she goes." Josie's mother sighed again. "That's the least we can do for old Faith, after all the years of willing service she's given us."

Mrs. Grace got up and went to fill the kettle. She put it on the stove and then stood staring out of the kitchen window. Josie watched her, realizing how unusual it was to see her mother stay still for any length of time. She was always on the go, full of ideas and energy. Josie noticed her mother's faraway expression and the worry lines that creased her forehead and felt a sudden pang of guilt. She'd been so wrapped up in herself, she hadn't spared much time to think about how anyone else might be feeling. And her mom loved Faith just as much as she did. Josie walked over and, putting an arm around her mother's neck, rested her head on her shoulder for a minute.

Mrs. Grace patted her hand. "You're getting to be as tall as I am," she said.

"What are you thinking about, Mom?" Josie asked gently.

"About the day I found Faith," she answered, smiling. "At the gymkhana. Come on, I've told you the story more than a dozen times."

"Tell me again," said Josie. She was never tired of hearing how the first horse had come to Grace's Riding Stables.

"Well, your dad and I had just moved to School Farm. I tell you, Josie, it was like a dream come true when we found this place and it looked like I could open my own stables at last," Mrs. Grace said, tearing her gaze away from the window and reaching for the tea. She threw some tea bags into the shiny brown tea pot. "There were six stalls, and I planned on keeping three or four horses, with perhaps a couple of horses at some stage in the future for riding lessons. You weren't born then, but we wanted to have a family and it was the ideal way for me to work and look after a child." The kettle began to whistle, so she took it off the stove and filled up the pot. Josie unhooked a couple of mugs from the shelf and took a flowery china milk jug out of the refrigerator.

"Well," Mrs. Grace continued as she poured the tea, "I wanted to get to know some horsey people, so

I went to the gymkhana to see what was going on. And then I saw Faith, in the pole bending race. I couldn't take my eyes off her!" She passed a steaming mug to Josie and then blew on the other one, smiling at the memory. "She was trying so hard, though the boy who was riding her was much too big and heavy. I got talking to his mother, and she said they had just decided to sell Faith and buy a new horse. Faith was the ideal first horse, she said, very good with beginners. She seemed perfect, and I loved her name—so quiet and trusting, somehow. It really suited her."

Mrs. Grace reached across for the cookie tin before continuing. "Anyway, then I found out how much money the owners wanted for her," she said, offering the tin to Josie. "We had nowhere near enough, and it made me think I'd have to shelve the whole idea for a while. I was going home afterward, feeling down and miserable, when there she was, stuck in traffic in the trailer in front of my car! She was poking her head out of the back and looking at me as if to say, *Well, here I am. What are you going to do about it?* We looked at each other for five minutes and then I got out of the car and offered her owner most of our savings, plus so much a month for the rest of the year. And, amazingly enough, she agreed!"

"And Dad was furious at first, but he forgave you as soon as he set eyes on her," Josie finished off, munching on her cookie, "and Faith was your anniversary, birthday, and Christmas present all in one."

"That's right," laughed her mother. "But I hid her in the stables for a whole day and a half before I got up the courage to tell your father. She soon began to earn her keep, though. There must be hundreds of children around here who've learned to ride on Faith. Anyway, that's all in the past, now. I'm afraid it's time to look to the future."

She lapsed into an unhappy silence. Basil sat against her leg, looking up at her with adoring brown eyes, and she gently stroked one of his soft ears.

"You have another cup of tea, Mom," Josie said. "I'll turn Faith out into the field."

"Thanks, Josie," her mother said gratefully. "I've untacked her, so you just need to pick out her feet."

"Okay, Mom," Josie replied, running up to her room to change into jeans and a sweatshirt.

Across the yard was a row of six roomy stalls,

and Faith was waiting patiently in the first one. Since the weather was getting milder, the horses were left out overnight and the Graces' other two horses, Hope and Charity, were already in the field. The three boarder horses were grazing in the other paddock: Captain, a bay hunter, Tubber, a skewbald belonging to another teacher at Mr. Grace's school, and Connie, a beautiful black mare who was Mary Grace's own particular favorite.

"Hello, there, old girl," Josie called softly as she let herself into Faith's stall. There was an answering whinny as Faith came to greet her, nuzzling against Josie's shoulder. She had a dark bay coat, with a white stripe on her face and four white socks. Josie reached into her jeans pocket and pulled out a peppermint. She held the mint out on the flat of her palm, and Faith crunched it happily, tossing her head up and down a few times in appreciation. Josie took a hoof pick out of the grooming kit that was kept in the stall. Bending over, she slid her hand down one of Faith's legs, picked up her foot and ran the hoof pick around it to clean out the sand and dirt.

It was peaceful, working quietly away in the sweet-smelling stable, and Josie decided to give Faith

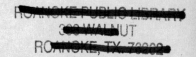

a quick rub with the body brush. Drifts of loose hair came away with each stroke. Faith was losing her rough winter coat now that spring had arrived.

"That'll make you more comfortable, old girl," Josie said as she dealt with the matted clumps on the mare's chest and belly. She loved spending time with the horses, and she knew how much they loved being groomed. Having something practical to do took her mind off all the anxiety, too, and made her feel calmer about what the future might bring.

"You're not worried, are you, Faith?" she said as she brushed with steady strokes. "You'll just accept whatever happens and deal with it in your own way, won't you? Well, I'm going to try and do the same."

By the time she had finished with Faith and was leading her out of the stable, dusk was falling. A pair of headlights lit up the shadows as a car came slowly up the drive and parked in the yard. Josie's father got out of the driving seat and waved at her.

"Hi, Dad," she called. "How was your day?"

"So-so," he replied, walking over. "Tenth-graders are finding *Romeo and Juliet* a struggle, and I've got a pile of grading to do." Robert Grace had never taught at any of the schools Josie attended, much to her relief. She liked to keep her home life quite separate. "How are you?" he added, taking a look at his daughter's very solemn face.

"Not great," Josie replied. "Faith's advertisement went in the paper today. It's on the kitchen table, if you want to see it. Somehow, it makes the whole thing seem real. I always thought something would crop up at the last minute and we wouldn't have to move, but it's not going to, is it?"

"I'm afraid not, sweetheart," said Mr. Grace sadly. "But I bought a lottery ticket today—after all, miracles can sometimes happen!" He scratched Faith's white stripe and she blew down her nose at him in her usual friendly way. "Dear old Faith," he said. "It'll be strange without her."

For a while the three of them stood quietly together in the gloom, and then Mr. Grace said, "Look, Josie, I understand how difficult this is for you and your mother. If there was anything I could do to change things, I would."

"I know, Dad," Josie said. "But I've been thinking it over, and I'm going to try and make the best of things—just like Faith does. She's so quiet and trusting. I think she knows we won't let her down.

And anyway, we'll probably still be able to see her in her new home, won't we?

"I'm sure we will," said Mr. Grace, ruffling her hair. "Somewhere, there's bound to be someone who'll care for her and love her just as much as we do. Don't worry—we'll find them!"

CHAPTER TWO

Josie led Faith across the yard and toward one of the fields beyond the outdoor schooling ring. "Shoo, there!" she said, as a couple of ducks waddled in front of her on their way back from the small pond that lay between the fields. She opened the gate and walked the horse through, closing it securely behind her. Then she took off Faith's bridle, knowing she would have no problem catching her again. "Off you go!" she said, giving her a farewell pat on the shoulder.

Faith stretched out her neck and shook her mane, then ambled around the paddock for a while, then trotted off to join Hope and Charity.

Josie smiled as she saw the three horses greet

each other, and sat on the gate to watch them for a while. They sniffed noses and exchanged a few playful nibbles, then Faith led the other two in a sweeping circle around the paddock. Hope's light gray coat shone out in the dusk, with the larger shadow of Charity beside her. Even Josie had to admit that Hope was not the most beautiful horse in the world. She had a long, straight face with rather small eyes, and an especially broad back. Those shortcomings were more than made up for by her sweet nature, though. She was a calm, gentle, and affectionate horse. Her daughter Charity had a slightly darker coat and a more attractive face, with intelligent, expressive eyes. Every visitor to Grace's Stables fell in love with her instantly, and she was always in great demand for lessons.

Josie sighed as she looked at the horses together. They would miss each other just as much as she was going to miss them. Then suddenly, she felt two hands come around her waist from behind and squeeze, digging in just below her ribs. "Hey!" she cried, laughing and nearly falling off the gate. "Anna!" Turning around, she saw her friend's smiling face and immediately felt better. Anna had such an infectious grin, it was hard to feel sad when her smile beamed her way.

"I've come to cheer you up," Anna announced, digging into her jacket pocket and pulling out a packet of potato chips. "Your mom told us you were out here."

"Oh, thanks, Anna, you're the best," Josie said, helping herself to the open packet which Anna was waving in front of her nose. "Is Ben here too?"

"Yes, he's saying hello to Tubber," Anna replied, pointing toward the other field. Her brother was just opening the gate while Tubber trotted across the grass to meet him, whinnying in greeting. Josie watched as he made a big fuss of the friendly skewbald. The other two horses kept as boarders, Captain and Connie, raised their heads for a moment to watch, and then continued grazing.

"Ben just loves that horse," Josie commented as she munched her way through a handful of chips. "I hope Mrs. Collins can find somewhere close by to keep him."

Tubber was one of the first horses to be boarded at the stables, fourteen years before. His owner, Mary Collins, was a busy teacher at the school where

Josie's father worked. She only had time to ride him on weekends, so Ben had begun to help Mrs. Grace exercise Tubber after he and Anna had learned to ride. Mrs. Grace had given them free lessons in return for their help around the stables on weekends. Most of the children she taught had their lessons on Saturday or Sunday, apart from a few who came after school during the week, so there was always plenty to be done.

"Oh, I think Ben would ride his bike for miles to take care of Tubber," Anna said, smiling. "Now, come on, tell me everything."

"Well, the ad for Faith *is* in today's paper," Josie replied, "but no one's called yet. And Mom's told a few people whose children come for lessons that we're selling her."

"I bet you'll get loads of offers," Anna said, watching Faith as she grazed in the paddock. "She's such a sweetheart."

"I know, but she's quite old," Josie said seriously. "We need to find someone who understands the kind of care she needs and won't expect her to go riding for miles every day. It's not going to be easy."

Anna nodded in agreement. "I don't know how

you're going to be able to say good-bye to Faith. You've known her all your life, after all. It'll be like losing one of the family! Oh, sorry," she said, catching sight of Josie's expression. "I'm not doing a very good job of cheering you up, am I? What I was really coming over to say was that Ben and I are going to Dad's this weekend, but we're not leaving until Saturday. So, why don't the three of us take the horses for a ride after school on Friday? Come on, Josie—it'll be fun! After all, it might be our last chance, you know. The three of them aren't going to be together for very much longer."

"Anna! Stop talking about it, for goodness' sake!" Josie exclaimed. "I'm going to get you back!" She jumped off the gate and started chasing her friend around the pond. Within a few minutes they were both giggling as Anna gasped, "Sorry, sorry, sorry! I'm trying to be honest!"

"Well, you'd better try a bit harder," Josie replied, flopping down on the grass. "It's difficult enough putting on a brave face, without you reminding me how awful everything is the whole time."

"Okay, point taken," Anna said, sitting beside her. "Blame it on stress. We're meeting Dad's new girlfriend this weekend, and I'm not exactly looking forward to it."

"No, I bet you're not," Josie said sympathetically. She knew how difficult Ben and Anna found the weekends away at their father's. Mike Marshall had stayed in the city when he and his wife had separated and Ben and Anna went to spend the weekend with him once a month. The visits were not always happy ones, though their father tried his best to make them a success.

"It's just that we don't really know anyone there anymore," Anna said, watching a bossy coot chase a mallard duck across the water. "We'd rather be hanging out with our friends or helping you here than watching videos in Dad's apartment all day."

"Come on," Josie replied, scrambling to her feet and holding out a hand to pull Anna up. "I think a ride on Friday is just what we all need. Let's do it! And can you and Ben stay for supper tonight?"

"Yes, please," said Ben, looming up out of the shadows beside them. "We left Mom a note, just in case you invited us."

"Great," Josie smiled. It was funny how often Ben and Anna appeared at mealtimes, but the Graces were always happy to see them—and to feed them.

"It's no trouble—Rob always cooks too much anyway," Mrs. Grace would say, laying a couple more places at the table. Josie's father liked to relax after a hard day at school by trying out some new recipe—the more complicated, the better. He was happy to spend hours chopping up vast quantities of vegetables, while the kitchen windows clouded over with steam from the various pots bubbling away on the stove. This evening, an enticing smell was wafting out from the house.

"Mmm, get a load of that garlic," Ben said, wrinkling his nose in appreciation. "Your dad's a great cook, Josie—you are lucky."

"I know," Josie replied, looking at the peaceful scene as they walked back toward the house. The last few chickens and ducks were making their way to the hen house for the night, and she made a quick detour to close the door behind them, safe from the foxes. Across the yard, their two black-and-white cats, Millie and Rascal, were playing in the straw by the open barn doors, and Basil was snuffling around one of the empty stalls. Josie had lived here all her life, with animals everywhere and horses in the field below her bedroom window. How could she possibly move anywhere else?

"I bet you feel really awful about having to leave the cottage, as well as the stables closing down," Anna said, as though she could read Josie's mind.

"Anna!" Ben exclaimed, glaring at his sister.

"Oh, it's okay, Ben," Josie told him. "I'm getting used to her by now. It's kind of like shock therapy, having your nose rubbed in how awful everything is."

"All right, all right! I get the message," Anna said, holding up her hands in surrender. "I won't mention it again, I promise."

"Hello, there," Mr. Grace said to Ben and Anna as they trooped into the kitchen. "Mary told me you were around, so I've counted you in for supper. Okay?"

"Yes, please," Anna said.

"Something smells great!" Ben added. "What is it?"

"Spaghetti with an amazing sauce of my own invention," Mr. Grace replied. "We're nearly ready— I just need someone to make a salad and someone to set the table."

Five minutes later, Josie had set the table with five places and put in the middle a rather odd-looking salad that Ben and Anna had helped put together from all sorts of leftovers in the fridge. Thick chunks of cucumber, cold peas, and some mandarin orange pieces were scattered over the lettuce leaves, and they had garnished the whole thing with slices of salami. "Very artistic," Mr. Grace said with a smile as he dished up the spaghetti. "Give your mother a shout, could you, Josie?"

Mrs. Grace came in from the study. "One day I'm going to disappear and you'll eventually find me under a huge pile of paperwork," she said, pulling out a chair and sitting down. "So, you two, how's your mother? I haven't seen her for ages."

"She's really busy on this decorating job," Anna said, passing down a plateful of pasta. "It was nearly finished, and then the woman didn't like the wallpaper in the hall, so Mom had to strip it off and start all over again."

Lynne Marshall really wanted to be a full-time artist, but that didn't bring in enough money, so she worked as a painter and decorator to keep the family going. She and Mary Grace were nearly as close as Josie and Anna. "Lynne doesn't have an easy time of it," Josie had heard her mother say to her father in private the other day. "It makes me realize how lucky I am, in spite of everything."

"Oh no," Mr. Grace groaned as the phone rang just when they were all about to start eating. "Let's ignore it—it'll stop eventually."

"We can't, Rob," his wife reminded him, getting up. "It might be someone calling about Faith."

Josie put down her fork, her stomach sinking and her mouthful of food suddenly hard to swallow. She strained to hear what her mother was saying in the hall outside, and caught the words ". . . good with children . . . yes, very placid . . ."

Anna opened her mouth to say something, then shut it again quickly as she caught Josie's eye. They continued eating—or trying to—in silence, until Mrs. Grace said good-bye to whoever was on the other end of the phone and replaced the receiver with a final click. After a short pause, in which everyone could have heard a pin drop, she came back into the kitchen.

"Well?" Josie said, unable to restrain herself. "Who was that? It *was* about Faith, wasn't it?"

"Yes, it was," her mother replied, with an expression that was hard to read on her face. "That was Juliet Henderson. You know, Jerry's mother."

26

"The red-headed boy?" Anna said. "With about fifty little brothers and sisters?"

"That's the one," Mrs. Grace said. "Come on, though, there are only three of them, I think. It just seems like more because they're all so . . ." She let the sentence hang, searching for the right word to describe the Henderson children.

"Mom, we couldn't let Faith go to the Hendersons," Josie said. "Do you really think they'd look after her?"

"Well, I couldn't just say no," Mrs. Grace said. "We've got to investigate every possibility, and the Hendersons have got a field, and some kind of a stable. Mrs. Henderson's very eager for us to have a look at it, and I couldn't really refuse. We ought to give them a chance, at least. If the place isn't suitable, we can put them off and, if it is, we can have a good chat with them about looking after Faith. They seem very determined—Mrs. Henderson told me to name the price."

"It seems strange to be thinking about money in exchange for Faith," Mr. Grace commented. "Like selling one of the family. I wonder how much we would get for Josie?"

"Thanks very much, Dad!" Josie said, flicking a pea at him.

"Don't worry, dear," Mrs. Grace told her, "I'll advertise your father first, though I don't know how many offers we'd get."

"Oh, we'll take him," Anna said. "He can be our housekeeper, and cook for us every day. We'll keep him in the living room and let him sleep on the sofa."

The shrill ring of the phone cut short their laughter, and Mr. Grace sighed. "I think I'd better put your plate in the oven, Mary," he said. "It looks like we're in for a busy evening."

CHAPTER
THREE

It *was* a busy evening, and by the end of it, there had been seven phone calls from people interested in looking at Faith. Some of them were parents of children who were taught at the riding stables and one girl, Emma Price, was due to ride Faith the next day.

By the time the lesson was under way, Josie was sitting upstairs in her bedroom after another long day at school. She was trying to concentrate on her homework and resist the temptation to look out of the window.

"Now, Emma, I want you to change the rein," she could hear her mother say. "When you get to the letter H, go left across the arena to F, and turn right. Shorten your reins a little now, to get a better contact."

Josie had been hearing phrases like that all her life—she often thought she could give a riding lesson in her sleep, though she knew she wouldn't be as patient as her mother.

"Prepare to turn now," Mrs. Grace was saying. "Shorten your left rein and squeeze with your right leg. *Right* leg, Emma, the one next to the fence. Get Faith to move her whole body when she turns, not just her head."

Josie couldn't bear it any longer. She put down her pen and leaned on the windowsill to watch what was going on, resting her chin on her hands. Her mother was in the middle of the ring, dressed in her usual uniform of dark polo neck and stretch jodhpurs. From a distance, she looked almost as young as Josie, with her curly brown hair and slim figure. Emma was having a lesson on her own and, from the look of it, her mind was on other things. She guided Faith along a meandering line to the letter F on the other side of the arena fence. Once there, though, she left it too late to ask the horse to turn right, so they had a very sharp corner to negotiate.

"Can't we do some cantering now?" Josie heard her ask. "This is boring!"

"Look, Emma, there's more to riding than cantering," Mrs. Grace replied. "You've got to control Faith, get her listening to what you're saying. She's drifting around all over the place because you're not giving her clear instructions. Just trot a twenty-meter circle for me on the right rein and really try to remember everything I've been telling you. Then we can finish off with a quick canter, if you like."

"Great!" said Emma, brightening up. "That's more like it."

"Shorten those reins and prepare to trot," said Mrs. Grace. "Now, trot!"

Josie watched as Emma eventually managed to get Faith into a halfhearted trot, leaning forward with her reins flapping over the horse's neck. She was unbalanced and her weight was all at Faith's front end, so that the horse's hind legs were not moving as actively as they should.

"Sit tall!" said Mrs. Grace. "Take up your reins and keep your legs long. That's better!" Gradually, with lots of patient encouragement, Emma got herself together into a more balanced position, and she and Faith began to move together in harmony.

"Look, you're even on the right diagonal," said Mrs. Grace. "See? You're sitting down in the saddle as Faith's right leg goes forward. Well done! That looks so much better."

"I'm doing it!" Emma cried. "This is great!"

"Faith will do whatever you ask her," Mrs. Grace said. "You've just got to make sure you're giving her the right signals. Now, she's trotting well and you're in a good position to move to a canter. At the next corner, take up contact, sit down in the saddle, and squeeze with your legs. Outside leg behind the girth, remember."

Josie walked over to the schooling ring just as Emma was finishing her canter, her eyes shining and her cheeks pink with effort. She said hello to Mr. Price, who was sitting on a tree stump watching his daughter's progress, then opened the gate and walked alongside Faith as Emma rode her back into the yard.

"Good lesson?" she asked, though the answer was obvious.

"It was wonderful!" Emma replied. "Faith's the best horse ever. I think I could canter on her forever!"

"Well, she's due for a rest now," Mrs. Grace

replied. "Hop down and hold her for a minute while Josie takes off her saddle. I'll go and book you in for the same time next week."

Josie ran up the stirrup straps and unbuckled Faith's girth, heaved off the saddle and took it to the tack room. She came back with a rug that she threw over Faith. Emma stood holding the horse's reins, telling her father just how wonderful she was.

"I'm really making progress, Dad," she said excitedly. "If Faith was my own horse I could ride her every day, and canter for miles. We could enter Horse Club shows—maybe even go hunting!"

Josie looked up in alarm, uncertain whether to interrupt. Luckily, her mother was walking back from the office and had overheard what Emma was saying. "Now, hold on a minute," she told the Prices good-naturedly. "I don't want to bring you down to earth with a bump, but I'm afraid Faith's hunting days are over. She's quite an old lady now, you know, and she just can't handle too much exercise."

"But if Emma's happy on her," said Mr. Price, "that's the main thing, isn't it? We want to find a horse we can trust, and Faith seems to fit the bill perfectly. We could board her over in Littlehaven, and Emma could ride her every day after school. Then she could canter to her heart's content! Just tell us what kind of sum you're looking for and I'm sure we can match it."

Josie took the reins from Emma, seething inwardly. Of course Emma's being happy isn't the main thing! she felt like saying. It's whether Faith is being well cared for that matters.

"I'm sorry, Mr. Price," her mother said firmly, "but I think Faith is really too old for the kind of riding Emma has in mind. She's nearly ready to retire now."

"Well, what if I doubled the highest bid you've had so far?" Mr. Price said, with a wink. "I bet that would make you change your mind!"

Josie was taken aback and, for a moment, her mother seemed lost for words. "Look, Mr. Price," Mrs. Grace said eventually, "our main priority is finding Faith a home where she'll be happy and looked after in the right way. It's time for her to start taking things easy and I don't think she's the right horse for Emma. Really, it wouldn't be right for either of them."

* * *

"What a strange man," Mrs. Grace said to Josie as they led Faith back to her stall. "Thinking it was all a question of money. Couldn't he hear what I was saying to him? Faith's a wonderful horse to learn on, but we couldn't let her go to some young girl who'd want to ride her all day, every day. Emma's really becoming a good rider now, but she's quite impatient. I'm sure she wouldn't be happy with Faith for long."

"We won't let Emma get hold of you, don't worry," Josie told Faith, opening the stall door and leading her inside. Mrs. Grace shut the lower half of the door behind them and Josie began to unbuckle her bridle.

"There is another possibility, though," Mrs. Grace said carefully, leaning over the door. "I had a phone call today from Jane Randall, Isobel's mother. You remember Isobel, don't you? She had lessons here for a while a few years ago."

"Oh, yes, I do," Josie said, hanging the bridle over her arm. "She was nice, wasn't she? A bit older than me."

"That's right," said her mother. "Well, the family's moving up to Scotland, apparently. Mr.

Randall's been offered this wonderful job and they've found a big house near Glasgow—with stables and a paddock."

Josie looked at her mother, horrified. "And?" she said. "Are they thinking of taking Faith all the way to Scotland?"

"Well, yes, they are," said Mrs. Grace, not wanting to meet her daughter's eye. "They're going to get a horse for Isobel's brother, and they thought Faith would be perfect for Isobel. She's a bit nervous, but she learned to ride on Faith and she trusts her completely. She's a sensible girl, and I know she'd look after Faith properly. And her parents think it would help Isobel settle in if she had a horse to look after."

"But what about Faith, going miles from home?" Josie burst out. "How would *she* feel about it? And how could we possibly keep in touch with her, so far away? We'd never see her again!" She was dangerously close to crying.

"I know, sweetheart, honestly I do," Mrs. Grace said soothingly. "It's only an idea at this stage. But it might turn out to be the best thing for Faith, and I don't think we should dismiss the offer without considering it very carefully. Now, I need a cup of tea—it's been hard work this afternoon. Are you coming back to the house?"

"No, I'll stay here for a while," Josie said, not meeting her mother's gaze. After she had gone, Josie leaned her head against Faith's smooth neck and closed her eyes as she breathed in the warm horsey smell. "You can't go up to Scotland, I won't let them take you!" she whispered, but Faith just turned away and ambled over to the hay.

Letting herself back out of the stall, Josie was startled to hear the impatient beep of a car horn. An immaculate, shining large car was parked in the middle of the yard. Standing beside it was an equally immaculate sandy-haired man in a tweed jacket and neatly pressed trousers.

"I'd like to see whoever's in charge, please," he announced when he saw Josie appear.

"Um, okay," said Josie, slightly startled. "That'll be my mother, Mary Grace. I'll get her for you. Can I tell her what it's about?"

"I think I'm the best person to do that, wouldn't you say?" the man replied. He looked coldly at Josie with pale blue eyes underneath bushy eyebrows.

"You run along and get her for me, and I'll take over from there. I'll wait for her right here."

Josie felt the color rise in her cheeks. The man hadn't exactly been rude, but he'd put her very firmly in her place. It was clear he thought explaining anything to her would be a complete waste of breath. "I won't be long," she said, walking off toward the house. When she came back to the yard with her mother, the man was pacing up and down beside the car, looking at his watch.

"There you are at last," he said when he saw Mrs. Grace. "I don't have very much time to spare this afternoon."

"And you are?" Mrs. Grace asked, raising her eyebrows.

"The name's Philip Hyde-White," the man replied. "Won't beat around the bush. Saw your advertisement in the paper—elderly mare, needing a good home. Well, if she's what I'm looking for, I can give her the best home she'll find around here. You can be sure of that." And he smiled—a very self-satisfied smile, Josie thought. She turned his name over in her mind; it sounded vaguely familiar, though she couldn't quite work out why.

"And what *are* you looking for?" Mrs. Grace said.

"A good companion for my other horses," Mr. Hyde-White said. "Got a pair of two-year-olds I'm bringing up. Lots of potential, but they need a mature animal around to show them how to behave, and my old hunter died last month. A shame. We do have a couple of older horses as well, but they're not much use. My daughter, Hatty, has got a temperamental horse, and my wife's horse is an antisocial creature. Your mare might be just right. You say she's got no vices?"

"Absolutely none," Mrs. Grace replied. "She's very good-tempered, easy to catch and shoe, quiet to handle."

"And how's her health?" he asked sharply. "Does she suffer from arthritis?"

"We haven't seen any signs so far," said Mrs. Grace. "She's stumbling a little, but the vet's checked her over and says she's basically fine."

"I'll take a look at her, then," said Mr. Hyde-White. "Where is she?"

"She's in her stable at the moment," said Mrs. Grace calmly, but Josie could tell by the way her mother had drawn herself up to her full height and squared her shoulders that she was beginning to find Philip Hyde-White rather irritating.

"Well, why don't you get your girl to ride her around the arena?" he said. "I don't have much time, as I said, but I'll be able to tell very quickly if it's worth taking this any further."

"I'd be happy for my daughter to trot Faith around the yard on the leading rein, but I'm not going to saddle her up again," said Mrs. Grace firmly. "She's been working hard today, and she needs a rest."

"But I wanted to see her put through her paces!" said Mr. Hyde-White indignantly.

"Then you should have called first and made an appointment," said Mrs. Grace, returning his gaze with an equally steely one of her own. "If you'd like to come back at another time which is convenient for both of us"—and she emphasized the "both"—"then we can certainly let you have as much time as you want with Faith."

There was a short silence as Mr. Hyde-White stared at the determined woman in front of him. Mary Grace was quite short, but she had a natural air of authority about her that worked as well on people as it did on horses. She didn't need to raise her voice: one look from those clear gray eyes was just as effective.

"All right," he said abruptly. "Just bring her out here and I'll see whether I need to come back again. Take your point. Don't want to overtire her."

Round one to you, Mom, Josie thought to herself as she took a bridle and lead rope from the tack room and went to get Faith.

"Here she is," said Mrs. Grace proudly when they appeared. "This is Faith. I bought her locally when she was eight, and she's been with us for fourteen years. She's absolutely as steady a horse as you'll find."

Josie looked at Mr. Hyde-White, ready to jump to Faith's defense if he began to criticize her. She couldn't bear the thought of anyone not liking their beloved horse. True, Faith was getting on a bit, but surely it was obvious what a darling she was, standing so patiently there in the yard. She carried her head proudly, and she had an alert, intelligent expression in her shining brown eyes.

Luckily for him, Mr. Hyde-White seemed to appreciate Faith's finer points. "Holds her head nicely," he said approvingly. He went up to the mare and patted her quietly, taking a look at her teeth with a practiced eye. All the bluster seemed to have gone out of him as he concentrated on the horse in front of him, and it was clear he was enjoying getting to know her. He ran his hands down each of Faith's legs and checked one of her hooves.

"I should imagine the horse's not going to need too much exercising?" he said, watching closely while Josie walked her up and down the yard.

"No, we're cutting down on the amount of work she does," Mrs. Grace agreed. "That's why we don't want her to go to someone who'll want to ride her into the ground."

Of course! Josie said to herself as she led Faith smartly along. I know who his daughter is—Harriet Hyde-White! No wonder the name sounded familiar. And she looks just like him.

"Mom," Josie said as they watched Mr. Hyde-White pull out of the yard in his big shiny car, "I know his daughter, Harriet! She used to come to the Horse Club when Anna and I were going. Remember?"

"That would be about a couple of years ago now,"

Mrs. Grace said. "What was she like? Can she ride?"

"Oh, perfectly," Josie groaned. "She had this little bay horse and they used to win all the competitions, hands down. She always looked immaculate, too." She cast her mind back and pictured Harriet Hyde-White cantering around the ring, her strawberry-blond hair in a thick braid and her shirt a dazzling white. "She was a bit stuck-up, though," she added. "She never talked to anyone, and she was really mean to Anna once."

"Well, maybe she's like her father," Mrs. Grace said. "I think he finds animals easier to deal with than people. He really warmed up once he'd met Faith, though, didn't he? I was ready to swing at him until then, but maybe he's not so bad. And he certainly knows his stuff."

"Huh!" said Josie. "I'm not convinced. 'Get your girl to ride her around the arena.' How charming!"

"I know, I know," said her mother, chuckling. "I had to swallow hard a few times, I can tell you. But the important thing is whether Faith would be happy with the Hyde-Whites. And if the setup's anything like he says, I think we should give him the benefit of the doubt. Anyway, we'll soon have a chance to find out. He's invited us over next Monday afternoon—they're away over the weekend, apparently. Harriet won't be there, but we can see the stables."

"Well, I suppose there's no harm in looking," said Josie, relieved to hear that at least Harriet wouldn't be around to inspect them at the same time.

"No," agreed her mother. "Besides, they live at Littlehaven Hall. I've always wanted to have a look at that house. They opened the gardens to the public once, but I couldn't go. Everyone said it looked like a palace."

"Oh," said Josie, her heart sinking again. Faith in a palace? Somehow, she couldn't quite picture it.

CHAPTER FOUR

On Friday afternoon, the three horses and their riders clattered out of Grace's Riding Stables into the clear spring sunshine. They turned left on to the road, away from Northgate village and toward the open countryside. Josie breathed in the fresh air, smelling a faint trace of blossom on the breeze.

"Oh, it's good to be off for a ride on a day like this," she said, her eyes sparkling. "I was beginning to think it would stay gray and rainy forever."

On either side of them a patchwork of fields stretched out for miles, bright emerald with the young spring grass or chocolatey brown where the tractor had been plowing. Every so often, a powder puff of pink or white blossom burst out against the blue sky and dark green hedges. Everything looked bright and fresh, as though it had been washed clean. Faith was walking along with a spring in her step, her ears flicking back and forth alertly. It was the end of a long week, and Josie was determined to put all her problems behind her, for a few hours at least. She was off for a ride with her friends, and she was going to enjoy it.

"I think Hope feels the same way," Anna said, turning around to look back at Josie. "She's dancing along like a two-year-old." Often, Hope would lag behind when she had the chance, but today she was eager to be out.

Hope pricked up her ears in response to Anna's familiar voice, and she patted the light gray horse's neck affectionately. Mrs. Grace had taught Anna to ride on Hope when she and Ben had first turned up at the stables, three years before, and the plain, homely horse was still her favorite.

"She may not look like a million dollars, but I trust her," Anna always said. "And I know all her little ways. I know how she likes to be ridden, and she knows what I like. Not too fast and furious." Although Anna was much more bubbly and outgoing than Josie, she wasn't as confident on horseback. She'd fallen off a jumpy horse a couple of years before, and she still hadn't completely got her nerve back.

Josie usually rode Charity when the three of them went out riding, but today she'd chosen to take Faith. While she would never have put it as bluntly as Anna, she knew there probably wouldn't be many more chances to ride the old horse, and she wanted to grab every one that she could.

"Where shall we go?" Ben called from the front, on Charity. "Usual place? Do you think Faith could manage a canter?"

"She's only been out for a couple of lessons today, so she's quite fresh," Josie replied. "I think she'll be fine. Mom said they're plowing up the twenty-acre field, but if we keep to the edge we should be all right."

"Sounds good to me," Ben said, turning back again.

Josie smiled as she saw Charity take a bite at the hedge along the side of the road. You could tell Ben was used to riding Faith and Tubber, who were usually much better behaved. Charity would get away with as much as you'd let her.

A car whizzed quickly past them, and Josie saw Anna tense up. "Almost off the road now," she called, to reassure her. There was a fairly constant stream of traffic going by, but the horses were so well schooled they didn't pay it much attention. Fast cars and heavy trucks made Anna nervous, though, and Hope would be able to sense her anxiety.

"Getting off this road can't come too soon for me!" Anna replied. Josie watched her hold up a hand to thank a car that was now edging slowly past. Luckily, most of the drivers they met on the road were country people, who knew to pass the horses cautiously and give them plenty of room. And Mrs. Grace always insisted that riders wear fluorescent belts and armbands, so they could be clearly seen.

A few minutes later, they came to the field where they usually left the road. "I'll get the gate," Josie called, and Ben and Anna reined their horses back while they waited for Josie to open the gate. Josie leaned down from the saddle and grasped the gate firmly in one hand, while Faith walked slowly forward so that she could push it open. The bay horse was gate-opening champion at the riding school: she hardly needed any instructions from

Josie to wheel her hindquarters around gracefully while the gate was held open.

"Faith makes it look so easy!" Anna said as she and Hope followed Ben through. Charity had started fidgeting and stamping at the edge of the field, eager to be off.

"You go on," Josie called, seeing Ben was having trouble holding Charity back. "I'll catch up."

Carefully, Faith walked forward so that Josie could close the gate. Hope and Charity were already off, galloping along the edge of the big empty field. There was no one else in sight except a solitary tractor, turning over neat stripes of soil.

"Come on, girl!" Josie whispered, turning her around and giving the lightest squeeze of her legs against Faith's sides. With a snort of delight, the horse took off. She had a wonderful canter, smooth and balanced, and Josie felt as though she were sitting in a comfortable old rocking chair. She watched Faith's shoulder muscles ripple under her glossy coat, then held her face up to enjoy the sunshine and their graceful, leisurely pace.

Ben and Anna were standing waiting for them near the woods at the top of the field.

"Faith has great form!" Anna exclaimed as she watched Josie ride up. "She doesn't act her age, that's for sure."

"I know," Josie laughed, patting the horse's sweating neck. "Not quite ready for the retirement home, is she?"

They trotted along a quiet path at the top of the field, then cantered along a bridleway that led down to the river.

"I can't help worrying about Faith, though," Josie confided as they splashed along the shallow riverbed. "I can't bear the thought of her going somewhere she might not be happy."

"But your mother would never let that happen," Ben said, waving away a bumblebee that was humming around Charity's withers. "She'll make sure Faith has the best home she can find."

"I know," Josie said uncomfortably, "but it may not be easy to tell which the best home is." She drew Faith to a halt and they stood for a moment so that the horses could enjoy the cool water rippling over their fetlocks.

"What do you mean?" Anna said, squinting at her in the bright sunshine that bounced off the water.

"Well, a Mr. Hyde-White came to look at Faith the other day," Josie began, looking cautiously at her friend to see how this news would go down. She still hadn't quite worked out how she felt about the Hyde-White option for Faith. "You know, Harriet Hyde-White's father."

"What?!" Anna cried out so loudly that Charity shot out of the water and up the riverbank like a rocket. "You *can't* be thinking of letting Faith go to Horrible Harriet!"

"Whoa!" Ben yelled from the top of the bank, after he'd managed to get himself together and calm the horse down. "At least give us some warning if you're going to start shouting your head off!"

"Look, her father wasn't as bad as all that," Josie said. "He knows a lot about horses, and he's got a groom and fantastic stables. They wouldn't ride Faith very hard, and there would be other horses to keep her company. And they're local, so I'd still be able to visit her. There are some other people interested—but they want to take her up to Scotland and I'd probably never see her again! Nothing's been decided yet, though," she added hastily, as she noticed Anna's glowering expression. "We're going to look at the Hendersons' place tomorrow evening, and the Hyde-Whites' on Monday," she added, urging Faith up the riverbank to join Ben.

"But why do they want Faith in the first place?" Anna asked, looking up at them both. "She's not nearly posh enough for precious Harriet, is she?"

"Oh, come on, Anna! Are you and Hope going to stand in that river all day, or can we get going?" Ben called, as he and Charity began walking off.

"Apparently they need an older horse to show the young ones how to behave," Josie called back, following him along the top of the bank.

"Huh!" Anna snorted indignantly. "If you ask me, it's Harriet who needs to learn how to behave!" She and Hope scrambled up the bank and trotted to catch up with the other two. "I've never told you what she actually said to me at the gymkhana, have I?" she said, slightly out of breath.

"No," Josie said. "I only knew she'd been really nasty."

"I didn't want you to hear exactly how nasty!" Anna told her. "It was when Hope and I were the last ones left in that knockout jumping competition. Oh, what was that event called again?"

"Chase Me Charlie," Ben said automatically.

"Yes, that's it. Well, it was down to the two of us—me on Hope and Harriet on that little bay she had. She went past us with her nose stuck up in the air and said"—and here Anna lowered her voice, as though she didn't want Hope to overhear the hurtful remark—" 'It'll take more than a braided mane to make the creature *you're* on look halfway decent.' I could have jumped her!"

"How could she!" Josie gasped. She looked at Hope's honest, plain face. How could anyone be so unpleasant about such a sweet-natured animal? And what would Harriet say about Faith? That she needed to go to an old-age home for horses, probably.

"All that was a couple of years ago now, though," Ben said. "Maybe she's grown up a bit since then."

"Oh, don't be so nice about everybody!" Anna snapped. "Once a stuck-up snob, always a stuck-up snob. I wouldn't let Faith anywhere near her if I were you!"

CHAPTER
FIVE

"Listen, Josie," said Mary Grace. "I don't care *what* Harriet said to Anna two years ago at a gymkhana. The Hyde-Whites know all about looking after a horse like Faith. If the home they're offering is the best one for her, we should accept it—and gratefully, too."

It was early Saturday evening, and after a busy day at the stables, she and Josie were on their way to the Hendersons' house.

"I suppose we don't have to decide right away," Josie said, staring out of the car window as she thought it over. "Something else will probably turn up. Perhaps we'll see the Hendersons' place and think it'll be just perfect for Faith."

"I wouldn't hold out too much hope of that,"

said Mrs. Grace. "Still, I suppose you never know. Maybe we're being a bit hard on Jerry and his family. They might give Faith loads of love and attention." She yawned. "After a day like today, I'd rather be relaxing at home than running out to see them, all the same."

"I know what you mean," Josie said. "Saturdays seem to get busier and busier, don't they?"

"Not for much longer, though," Mrs. Grace replied. "We'll have to get used to a whole new kind of weekend soon. Just think, we may be able to sleep in once in a while. Pass me that piece of paper, would you? I think we're almost there."

"What will you do, Mom?" Josie said, as Mrs. Grace quickly consulted the scribbled directions she'd taken down over the phone. "You couldn't bear to give up horses altogether, could you?"

"I wouldn't mind a rest from teaching," Mrs. Grace admitted. "I think I'm getting a bit stale now. I'll continue riding Connie, though." Connie was the black mare who'd been kept at full board in the stables for the past eight years. Her owner had quickly become a good friend of Mary Grace's, and Mary had been riding Connie nearly every day for all that time. "Jane's going to move her to another boarding stable nearby soon," she went on, "but she's asked me to keep on exercising her. I'm sure there'll be lots of opportunities like that for you, too—if you want them."

"Hmm," Josie said, frowning. She couldn't imagine riding someone else's horse, and she didn't want to think about a future without the three they had. It was too painful. She had come to realize that the only way she could get through the next few weeks would be to take them one step at a time. Concentrate on Faith first, she told herself, and don't look too far ahead.

"Here we are," said Mrs. Grace, turning into a narrow driveway. "Now, brace yourself for the Hendersons!"

The car crunched over the gravel and drew to a halt outside a large, rather dilapidated house. Josie caught sight of a couple of faces at the window, and soon two red-headed boys and a little girl with carroty curls had spilled out of the front door and surrounded the car, all chattering at the same time. They wore strangely old-fashioned clothes: the boys were both dressed in corduroy knee britches and the girl in a pinafore of the same material, with a round-collared shirt beneath.

"Where's the horse? Why haven't you brought her with you? Come and see our stable! What's your name? How old are you?" they clamored, tugging at Josie's arm as she opened the passenger door.

"Now, children," came a slower, deeper voice behind them. "One at a time, remember?" A tall woman with long red hair came sailing toward the Graces, smiling serenely. Josie had seen her a few times, picking Jerry up from his riding lesson.

"Hello, Martha," she said to Mrs. Grace, and Josie had to bite her lip to stop herself from giggling. Mrs. Henderson obviously wasn't very good at remembering names. "The children have been simply dying for you to get here," she said. "Do come in, and bring . . ." Her eyes focused on Josie, and she waved her hand vaguely in the air to include her in the invitation.

"Josie, my daughter," Mrs. Grace added helpfully, as Josie was carried off toward the house by the tide of children.

"And what's your name?" Josie asked the little

girl, who was clinging on to her arm with a grip of steel and hustling her through the front door.

"I'm Jemima," she said. "And my one brother is Joshua and my other brother is Jerry. And our cat is called Chlöe, and she's had kittens. Look, there's one!"

By now, they'd reached the kitchen and, following Jemima's pointing finger, Josie saw that one of the faded flowery curtains seemed to be bulging and writhing, as though it were alive. Dragging a chair over to the windowsill, Jemima climbed up on it and began wildly tugging the curtain to and fro with a look of fierce concentration on her face.

"No, stop! I'll get her!" Josie cried, rushing up to the curtain and gently disentangling a tiny ginger kitten who was clinging desperately to the other side. She put the little creature down on the floor and it immediately took refuge under an armchair covered in threadbare red velvet, peeping out with big saucerlike eyes.

"And here's my guinea pig!" said either Joshua or Jerry, pushing a large wooden train along the floor. In the front sat a bemused-looking white guinea pig with pink eyes. "She's an albino and she's called Snowy."

"Animals and children, that's what we love," announced Mrs. Henderson, sweeping in with Mrs. Grace and scattering children and pets before her. "The more, the merrier! That's why we could give your dear old horse such a lovely happy home."

"That's my train!" came an angry cry from Jerry or Joshua, as one of the red-headed boys jumped on the other and began punching him. "Give it back!"

"No! Snowy likes it!" shouted the guinea-pig owner defiantly, defending himself with clenched fists.

"I think Snowy might like to go back in her cage now, don't you?" Josie suggested quietly to Jemima, pushing the train with its guinea-pig driver safely out of reach of flailing arms and legs.

"Snowy doesn't have a cage," Jemima announced loudly.

"No," said Mrs. Henderson, somehow overhearing above the din. "Lucky Snowy has a cozy cardboard box. Now, come on, Miriam. Let's leave the children playing and go out to the meadow." And, ignoring the chaos, she swept a speechless Mrs. Grace out through the back door.

"Why don't we put Snowy in her cardboard box for the moment," Josie said. "You know, I think we've got an old rabbit hutch in the barn. I could dig it out and Snowy could have that. What do you think?"

"What's wrong with her box?" Jemima said suspiciously. "I've drawn all over the side. Look!" And she proudly pointed to a large brown box covered in wax crayon scribbles in a corner of the kitchen.

"Those are lovely drawings," Josie said carefully, "but poor Snowy can't look out of her box and see what's going on, and it's not very strong. I think she might like the hutch better." She took Snowy out of the train and popped the poor bewildered creature into her box as a temporary shelter. At least it was clean, and there was a bowl of water and some lettuce leaves at the bottom.

"Now, come on, you two," she said cheerfully to the boys, who by now had stopped fighting and were both crying bitterly. "Are you going to show me the field?"

And so, along with cries of "I will! I will!" "No, she's *my* friend!" "But I have riding lessons and you don't!" "Well, I said it first!" she went out of the back door.

At the bottom of the overgrown garden was a small field, surrounded by a sagging barbed-wire fence. The two women were standing in the long grass, talking earnestly together. As Josie approached with the children, she heard her mother say "—a lot of work to make this field suitable for keeping a horse in, unfortunately. You've got ragwort everywhere."

"Yes, I'm so looking forward to seeing its pretty yellow flowers," said Mrs. Henderson. "We cut armfuls and make bouquets for the house—don't we, children?" But Jerry, Joshua, and Jemima had already rushed off shrieking, to climb through the window of what looked like a tumbledown garden shed.

"Ragwort's poisonous to horses, though," Josie added anxiously. "You'd have to dig up every last scrap."

"That's right," said her mother. "And there's a yew tree at the bottom of your garden, there, overhanging the fence. That would have to be cut right back—it's even more lethal. You'd need to repair the fence, too, or a horse would try to scratch on the barbed wire and could cut herself quite badly. And I'm afraid if that's the stable, it really won't give enough shelter."

"Oh, I'm sure any horse would love the stable!" cried Mrs. Henderson dramatically, shading her eyes to watch the children wriggling in and out of the gaping holes in its rotten sides. "It's so old. Quaint and picturesque, just how we like things to be!"

"Yes, but it doesn't have a roof," said Mrs. Grace. "That's quite a drawback."

"Well, there's obviously more to this horse-keeping business than I thought," Mrs. Henderson said, tossing her long red hair and preparing to sweep back to the house. "Perhaps Jeremiah would be better simply continuing with lessons for the time being. What do you think?"

"I think that might be best," Mrs. Grace agreed, adding tactfully, "He has the makings of a very good rider. I was going to try him over the trotting poles in the lesson tomorrow."

"And you could pick up the hutch then," Josie offered. Seeing Mrs. Henderson's blank look, she explained, "I was just telling Jemima, we've got an old rabbit hutch in the barn that would be perfect for Snowy. You'd be welcome to it, if you'd like. We don't need it anymore."

"An *old* hutch, you say?" Mrs. Henderson asked, raising an eyebrow.

"Oh, very old," said Josie. "Practically an

antique, and very picturesque." She coughed loudly, to cover up the strange snorting noise that her mother was making.

"Why, thank you, Josie dear," said Mrs. Henderson loftily. "What a kind thought. I think that would suit Snowy very well."

CHAPTER SIX

"I'm still booking people for lessons on Faith next week," said Mary Grace, up to her wrists in soapy water the next evening. "But we've got to face the fact that she might not be here for much longer."

"It'll take a little while to organize everything, right?" Josie asked, her heart sinking. She was standing next to her mother, drying the pots and pans. Because there were riding lessons throughout the day on a Sunday, the Graces always had a big dinner in the early evening. Mr. Grace cooked, and Josie and her mother cleaned up.

"Well, once we've decided which is the best home for her, there's no reason why things shouldn't move quickly," her mother replied. "I know the

Randalls are on a tight schedule with their move, and I think the Hyde-Whites don't want to drag the whole process out either."

Josie wiped away furiously at the saucepan in her hand, avoiding her mother's anxious glance. It was barely manageable to think of losing Faith at some time in the future, but not immediately.

"So how's it going so far?" Mr. Grace said, looking up from the Sunday papers that were spread all over the kitchen table. "Still a choice between the Hyde-Whites and the Randalls?"

Mary Grace nodded, sitting down at the table opposite him. "I've had a few more offers from families of some of the children I teach," she said, "but none really suitable. I'm beginning to realize it's not a question of money—talking to Emma's father made me see that."

"Oh, he was awful!" Josie said, trying to force a saucepan into the crowded cupboard. "As if doubling what we'd been offered for Faith would make any difference."

"Exactly! We've got to concentrate on getting the right home for her, not on what we can gain financially from the sale," said Mrs. Grace. "We have to find somewhere she can spend the rest of her days quietly and peacefully, with people who really know how to look after an elderly horse."

At that moment, there was a loud knock on the door. Basil leaped up from his basket under the kitchen table and started barking and leaping around in excitement.

"I wonder who that is?" Josie asked. "It can't be Anna and Ben—they're not back till late tonight."

"Oh, did I forget to tell you?" said her mother, getting up to answer the door. "The Randalls are coming over to talk about Faith. Maybe they'll be the answer to our prayers." She went to open the door, Basil at her heels.

"Yes, you did forget to tell me," Josie muttered, throwing down her napkin. "Still, I don't suppose it makes much difference."

"Now, come on, sweetheart," said her father, putting his arm around her shoulder. "Remember what you said about making the best of things?"

"Josie, why don't you and Isobel go and see Faith while it's still light out?" Mrs. Grace said, after she'd introduced the Randalls. Josie had recognized Isobel at once from her time at the stables—she had fair skin with a dusting of freckles and kind blue eyes.

"Great!" Isobel said at once. "I can't wait to see Faith again—I used to love riding her."

"Then let's go," Josie said, encouraged by the enthusiasm in Isobel's voice.

"Here! You might want to take these with you," said Mrs. Grace, throwing across a tube of peppermints to Josie. "We'll be out in a minute, after we've had a chat."

"Follow me," Josie said. "The horses are in the front field."

"How's Charity?" Isobel asked. "I remember when your mother was schooling her."

"Oh, she's wonderful," said Josie, her face lighting up as they walked over to the field. "She can be a bit stubborn sometimes, but she's really steady. All three of them are special, in their own way. Look, there they are!"

Hope and Charity were standing together in the middle of the field, Hope nibbling at her daughter's withers. Faith was grazing, a little way apart from them.

"Oh, Hope's doing her grooming routine again,"

Josie smiled. "She's fussy, but I think the others like it really."

"Faith's going to miss the other two," Isobel said, leaning on the fence and looking over at the peaceful group.

"I know," Josie sighed. "It's a funny thing, though—recently I've noticed she's been going off on her own a little more. I suppose it's because she's getting older. She seems to want some time to herself. Come on, take a few mints and let's go and say hello."

The two girls climbed over the fence and made their way across to the horses. Faith trotted up, giving a neigh and shaking her mane. Isobel patted her affectionately and in return, Faith nudged her nose into Isobel's shoulder.

"I think she remembers you," Josie smiled. "She doesn't do that with everyone she meets."

Isobel laughed as the horse nuzzled her pocket. "Or maybe it's just that she can smell these," she said, holding a peppermint out on the palm of her hand. "Oh, Faith, you haven't changed a bit—you're just as wonderful as you always were. And you don't look a day older."

"She is getting older," Josie said, watching as Faith crunched up the mint, tossing her head so that her mane rippled. "She's not picking her feet up quite as well as she used to, and she does get tired. Would you be wanting to ride her much?"

"No," Isobel replied thoughtfully, stroking Faith's soft nose. "I think we'd really be getting her more as a pet. I'd ride her sometimes, of course, but nothing too hard or competitive. My brother's crazy about horses and Mom and Dad have promised him a hunter, but that doesn't appeal to me. They don't want me to feel left out, though, and I suppose riding is a good way of meeting people."

Something in the tone of her voice made Josie look at Isobel more closely. "How do you feel about moving?" she asked, interested to find out more but not wanting to seem nosy.

"To be honest, I'm dreading it," Isobel sighed. "A new school as well as exams coming up, new friends to make, new house—new everything! I wish things could just stay the way they are."

"I know exactly how you feel," Josie said. She held out a mint for Charity, who was pushing her way forward to have a share in the attention. "We won't be moving as far away as you, but it still feels like my whole life's going to be turned upside down."

"Yes, I bet it does," Isobel said sympathetically. "I suppose taking Faith off to Scotland wouldn't be so good from your point of view, would it?"

"No, not really," Josie admitted. "But at the end of the day, I just want her to be happy. I'd rather she be with nice people up in Scotland than be miserable down here." Josie gave Isobel a halfhearted smile to show there were no hard feelings.

"Have you had any other offers?" Isobel asked, watching Faith trot off around the field.

"Yes, plenty," Josie replied, "though none of them have seemed right so far. But listen, here I am blabbering on and I haven't even offered to tack Faith up so you can ride her. Do you want to?"

"Oh, don't worry," Isobel replied, her eyes still fixed on Faith. "I've ridden her plenty of times in the past, and seeing her again is enough to remind me how perfect she is."

"Would you like to have her, if you could?" Josie asked. "I mean, if your parents and mine agree and the price is okay?"

"Yes," said Isobel slowly, "I would. I'd feel awful

about taking her so far away from you, Josie, but if she's got to go somewhere, I think she'd be as happy with us in Scotland as anywhere else."

Josie nodded. Maybe she would, she thought to herself. And maybe I'll just have to get used to it.

"Hi there, stranger!" Anna said, dropping her tray down next to where Josie was sitting on her own, in the school cafeteria. "Didn't you bathe this morning or are you just feeling antisocial?"

"Oh, Anna, it's great to see you!" Josie replied, beaming. "Seems like you've been away for a month. How was the weekend?"

Josie and Anna were in different classes, so this was the first chance they'd had to talk.

"How was the girlfriend, you mean," Anna said, taking a plate piled high with a burger and fries off the tray. "She wasn't as bad as I thought, as a matter of fact. It was a bit weird at first, seeing her with Dad, and I think he felt nervous, too. She's quite trendy. She took me and Ben shopping and bought us some cool clothes, which was nice of her, but Mom wasn't too pleased about all of our new purchases."

"Why not?" Josie asked, mashing butter into her baked potato.

"You know—'I'm the one who ends up buying the school shoes, why should they have all the fun?' etcetera, etcetera, etcetera. Oh, it's too boring to talk about," Anna said, with a bright tone in her voice that didn't fool Josie for one second. "How about you? What's happening with Faith? Has Harriet got hold of her yet?"

"Well, Mom and I are going over to their place tonight," Josie said, starting to eat. "Harriet won't be there—she's a weekly boarder at some private school or other—but we can have a look at the stables. We did see the Randalls, though. They're the people who are moving up to Scotland. Do you remember Isobel? She used to come to the stables a couple of years ago. Long hair, pretty."

"Oh yes," Anna replied, chewing slowly and thinking it over. "She used to ride Faith, didn't she?"

Josie had her mouth full, but she nodded.

"So, do they want to have her?" Anna asked.

"I think they do," Josie said. "Isobel seemed happy, and you can tell she really likes Faith. They said they'd talk it over and give us a call as soon as possible." She pushed some salad around her plate, not feeling quite so hungry all of a sudden.

"And how do you feel about it all?" Anna asked. "Would they give her a good home? Better than the Hyde-Whites?"

"They showed us pictures of the stables and field at their new house," Josie said. "It looks fantastic, and Isobel's brother's getting a horse too—so Faith wouldn't be lonely. And Mom likes them, and I'm sure they'd look after her well. It's just . . ." Her voice trailed away.

"It's just they're moving up to Scotland," Anna finished the sentence for her. "And you'd probably never see Faith again, and you couldn't ride Hope or Charity to visit her—while you've still got them, of course."

"Oh, Anna," Josie said, uncertain whether to laugh or cry, "how do you manage it?

"Manage what?" Anna asked innocently.

"Manage to put your finger on everything I don't want to think about and remind me of it," said Josie, pushing away her plate.

"Well, you've got to face up to things," Anna said briskly. "And I'm not going to let you mope around on your own. We're going to get through this together, the two of us, and Ben's going to help, too. That's what friends are for, after all." She gave Josie one of her dazzling smiles. "Can I have the rest of your potato if you don't want it?" she asked. "This burger is gross."

CHAPTER
SEVEN

Josie and her mother stared at each other for a moment without saying a word as they pulled up in the car outside Littlehaven Hall. Mrs. Grace turned off the engine and they took another look at the imposing building before them.

"What an amazing place!" Josie said, after a pause. "It looks like something out of a film. I never thought it would be as grand as this!"

"Me neither," said her mother. "You'd never guess it was here, tucked away down the drive like this, would you?"

They had turned off a main road between Northgate and the small market town of Littlehaven to find the house. It was built out of gray stone, and roofed in thick slate shingles of the same color. Circular columns supported a grand porch over the front door. Tall, rectangular windows looked out over a velvety lawn that was enclosed by the sweeping drive. It had been recently mowed in neat stripes. There was one flower bed in the middle of this green sea, spiked with roses, and a stone statue of a galloping horse nestled among trees at the far end.

There was something about the house that Josie didn't like. It's too perfect, and it's got a snobby air about it, she thought, as she gazed up at its gracious walls. Just like the Hyde-Whites.

"Come on," said Mrs. Grace, picking up her shoulder bag, "let's ring the bell before I lose my nerve."

A middle-aged woman in a uniform answered the door and said she would get Mr. Hyde-White for them. She walked softly away and left Josie and Mrs. Grace standing in the empty hall. Josie stared nervously at the gloomy oil paintings hung all around it, not feeling much like talking in that large, echoing space. It wasn't exactly welcoming.

"Hello, there," said a brisk voice, and Mr. Hyde-White appeared from one of the doors that led off the hall. He looked exactly the same as when he'd appeared at the stables—identical tweed jacket and sharply creased trousers. Josie tried to imagine him dressed in the jeans and sloppy sweaters her father wore on weekends, but she couldn't quite picture it.

"Glad you could make it," he went on. "Shall we go out to the stables right away? No point in wasting time."

He led them down a corridor and out through the back door, into a walled garden. Josie and her mother exchanged a quick smile as they followed behind him. It was obvious Mr. Hyde-White didn't believe in chatting for the sake of it. Still, at least that gave them the chance to look around, Josie thought. She noticed how neat and tidy everything was, from the stone urns precisely arranged on the terrace, to the straight, regimented rows of plants in the vegetable patch.

They continued down the path until Mr. Hyde-White stopped at a door in the far wall. "This is where we keep the horses," he said, throwing it open and standing aside to let them go past.

Josie walked through first. "Oh, what beautiful stables!" she said in delight.

A cobblestone yard lay in front of them, with two sets of stalls opposite each other on either side. Two horses were peering out of the left-hand row inquisitively. Across the yard, a handsome dun was tied with a rope from his bridle to a ring on the wall, while a young man in jodhpurs and a sweatshirt groomed him vigorously. The tidy muck pile was walled off in the far corner, and what looked like the storerooms for hay, feed, and bedding stood opposite. Beyond the courtyard, Josie could see an outdoor schooling ring, a paddock with a number of jumps in it, and then a sweeping view of fields and open countryside. She caught a quick glimpse of a woman on an iron-gray horse, moving slowly around the ring at a sitting trot.

"This all looks very well organized," Mrs. Grace said, sounding impressed.

"Yes, we run a tight ship," said Mr. Hyde-White proudly, squaring his shoulders. "Come on, I'll take you around. Introduce you to the residents."

Josie and her mother smiled uncertainly, not quite sure whether this was meant to be a joke. They followed Mr. Hyde-White over to where the dun horse was standing. The groom was just giving his beautiful glossy coat a final wipeover with the stable cloth.

"This is Milo, Hatty's gelding," said Mr. Hyde-White. "Stand back, David, so we can see him properly."

Without a word, the young man stood to one side at Milo's head. He didn't acknowledge the Graces or look at Mr. Hyde-White.

"She used to have a bay horse, didn't she?" Josie asked, walking up to the horse and cautiously giving him her hand to sniff.

"That's right," said Mr. Hyde-White. "Useful little thing, but Hatty grew out of her very quickly. She's on a different level with this fellow."

"He's got a lovely deep chest," Josie said, gently stretching out her hand. Milo shied away, laying his ears back against his head and rolling his eyes.

"He doesn't like strangers," Mr. Hyde-White replied. "Takes a lot of getting to know, but he's a super jumper—simply flies over the fences. Mind you, so he should. Cost me a small fortune." He gave a short laugh, without much humor in it. "You can put him back in his stall, David. Let's continue with the tour."

Briskly, he took Josie and her mother over to the other stalls and showed them the two-year-olds he was schooling: Jack, a chestnut stallion with a white star between his eyes, and Clementine, a palomino mare.

"We're working Jack every day on the lunge rein," he told Mrs. Grace. "He's got the makings of an excellent hunter, but he's a bit jumpy at the moment. That's why he needs a good role model to calm him down. A mother figure, you might say."

"And that's a nice-looking mare you've got," said Mrs. Grace, as Clementine stretched her neck over the stable door. "Doesn't she have a pretty head?"

"We're going to keep her as a brood mare," Mr. Hyde-White said matter-of-factly. "She has a great pedigree, but she's a devil to catch."

"She's gorgeous!" Josie exclaimed. She couldn't resist stroking the horse's soft nose, enjoying its whiskery tickle against her fingers, and patting her gleaming golden coat. Clementine drew her head back warily, but she didn't shy away completely.

"That's enough fussing," Mr. Hyde-White said sharply. "Now, come this way and we might be able to catch my wife before she finishes her dressage session."

Josie was taken aback. She'd never thought of stroking a horse as fussing—she knew how much they enjoyed being touched. Mr. Hyde-White obviously had a very different attitude. He marched off toward the arena and they had to hurry to keep up with him. As she went, Josie caught sight of the groom watching them go. She smiled, but he turned away.

The dark gray horse was going through its paces in the ring. His rider, a thin woman with short blond hair, sat deep in the saddle with a ramrod-straight back. She kept her eyes fixed ahead and didn't look once in their direction.

"I don't think you see this kind of thing very often in your neck of the woods," said Mr. Hyde-White, with a superior smile. "None of your pupils are up to dressage, I'd imagine."

"Oh, some of the adults are," Mrs. Grace replied. "One of our boarders regularly competes in dressage events, and I give his owner lessons."

"Probably not at my wife's level, though," Mr. Hyde-White said, looking rather smug.

"She certainly has a marvelous seat," says Mrs. Grace politely.

Mrs. Hyde-White hardly seemed to be moving at

all, but she obviously had complete control over her horse. His every movement was smooth and graceful, and he seemed simply to flow from one gait into another. Josie sometimes found watching dressage exercises rather boring, but she had to admit that there was something very beautiful about this perfectly balanced partnership of horse and rider.

"Look at that wonderful extended canter, Josie," said her mother, as the horse threw out his legs and lengthened his stride. "She's really got him moving his hindquarters so he doesn't overbalance. We ought to get Emma Price over to have a look at this!"

"We don't encourage spectators," said Mr. Hyde-White stiffly.

"Oh no, of course not," said Mrs. Grace hurriedly, quite flustered. "I was only joking. Oh, I think they've finished."

Mrs. Hyde-White had slowed her horse directly from a canter to a walk. She let her reins flap loosely so that he could give his neck a good stretch as they came out of the arena.

"This is Mary Grace, darling," said Mr. Hyde-White as she approached. He obviously didn't think Josie was worth mentioning. "You remember, she's looking for a home for her old mare. I think the horse will help settle my young ones."

"Oh yes," said Mrs. Hyde-White, languidly reaching down a hand so that Mrs. Grace could shake it. "Have you had a look around?"

"Yes, we have," said Mrs. Grace, forced to squint into the sun as she looked up at her. "The yard looks great. Tell me," she added, turning back to Mr. Hyde-White, "are you thinking of putting Faith out to grass right away?"

Josie looked around at the lush green fields. She had to admit, it was nice to imagine Faith spending the rest of her days grazing quietly in such peaceful surroundings.

"Oh, I think we could ride her every so often," Mr. Hyde-White replied. "David or Hatty can ride her and we'll see how she goes."

"Is she regularly shod?" Mrs. Hyde-White asked, flicking a blade of grass off one shining riding boot with the end of her whip.

Mrs. Grace nodded. "Every six weeks or so."

"Well, if her feet are in good condition and she's still wearing shoes, there's no reason why she shouldn't have some light work for a few years,"

Mrs. Hyde-White continued. "When we can fit her in."

"I could come and take her out if you didn't have the time," Josie offered, feeling she'd been left out of the conversation for long enough.

Mrs. Hyde-White stared down at her as though she'd just noticed an unpleasant smell and wanted to see exactly where it was coming from. "Oh no, dear, I don't think that will be necessary," she said.

"It might unsettle her," Mr. Hyde-White added. "Once the horse is here, better for her to be in our sole care, wouldn't you say?"

That wasn't what Josie would have said at all, but the tone of Mr. Hyde-White's voice was final. She glanced across at her mother with a look that said, *We need to talk about this later.*

"Well, you can work out the details," said Mrs. Hyde-White brusquely. "I need a hot bath and something to drink. Walk on, Jasper." And with that, she and her horse made their stately way back to the yard. Josie watched them go and saw Mrs. Hyde-White spring lightly to the ground, hand the horse's reins over to the groom, and walk toward the house without a backward glance. She didn't bother to give Jasper a pat of thanks or praise.

"Of course, before we give you the final decision about whether we'll take the horse," Mr. Hyde-White said, "we'll have to let Hatty have a look at her. She's away at school during the week, as I said, but we could make it on Friday evening. Then if she gives the go-ahead, we can arrange a time to pick the animal up. We'll pay your asking price. No point haggling. And I take it that covers her tack as well?"

"It would be fine for you and your daughter to come on Friday evening," Mrs. Grace said, "but I ought to mention that there is another family interested in Faith. They're thinking it over at the moment. We may decide that, for one reason or another, she might be happier with them in the long run."

Mr. Hyde-White stared at her. "I can't imagine for a moment why you would," he said. "You've seen our facilities. We have a very able groom, plenty of land, and a great deal of expertise. If I were you, I'd think very hard before turning this opportunity down."

Josie and her mother sat in the car without speaking as they drove away from Littlehaven Hall. Eventually, Mrs. Grace shot Josie a sidelong glance. "Well?" she said.

"Oh, Mom!" Josie replied. There was no need to say any more. She could tell her mother knew exactly how she felt.

Mrs. Grace sighed. "The thing is, he's right," she said. "We can't just dismiss their offer out of hand. Those are fantastic stables, and the fields look great, and there are other horses for company. And I'm sure the Hyde-Whites would look after Faith very well."

"But they're so cold!" Josie blurted out, clenching her hands so tightly that her fingernails dug into her palms. "Did you notice, Mom, he didn't call Faith by her name once! It was always 'the mare' or 'the horse' or 'the animal.' And he's not exactly affectionate with his horses, I don't think he touched one of them the whole time we were there."

"Of course, he doesn't look after them on a day-to-day basis," Mrs. Grace reflected. "I should imagine it's the groom who'd be doing that. And according to Mr. Hyde-White, he really knows his stuff."

"Well, I didn't like him either," Josie said. "He didn't say hello to us, or smile, and he didn't seem to like Mr. Hyde-White much. Come on, Mom—didn't you think there was something rather odd about that whole setup? I know it's an amazing place and everything, but can you really imagine Faith there?"

"Actually, I can," Mrs. Grace said slowly. "I think you're projecting your own feelings on to Faith, Josie. Just because you don't like the Hyde-Whites, you think she won't be happy living with them. Well, I'm not sure you're right. I can see her keeping those young horses in order and grazing on their land quite happily. And I can see the Hyde-Whites taking care of her as she gets older, too."

"Well, I can't," Josie said gloomily. "And once she goes there, that's it. We're not going to be invited back for a visit, you can count on that. Did you notice how horrified they looked when I offered to come and ride her?"

"Yes, they didn't exactly jump at the prospect, did they?" her mother smiled. She took one hand off the steering wheel and put it over Josie's. "Look, I can't deny that I liked the Randalls a hundred times better. They're much more friendly and on our wavelength. But Faith is the one we have to think about here, not ourselves. We've got to keep *her* best interests in mind. Let's wait and see what the Randalls say, and then we can decide."

Soon they were pulling into their driveway and past the field full of brightly colored fences and poles. "The Hyde-Whites had some marvelous jumps. Did you see?" Mrs. Grace asked Josie thoughtfully. "Like a proper show-jumping course. I must try a new layout for ours."

"There's not much point, is there?" Josie replied. "We're going to have to get rid of them all soon."

"Perhaps you're right," Mrs. Grace said reluctantly. Then she spotted her husband's red car in the yard and her face brightened. "Oh, look, Dad's home early. That's nice!"

"Is it really?" Josie said grumpily. She got out of the car and stomped up the path to School Farm, flinging open the front door with a crash.

Her father came out of the kitchen, alerted by the noise. "What's up with you?" he said, looking at Josie's cross face.

"Nothing—and everything," Josie muttered, taking off her jacket and jamming it on the post at the bottom of the stairs. "We've just been to see a wonderful new home for Faith, that's all. Can't wait to pack her off there."

"Now, come on," Mr. Grace said, putting his

hands on Josie's shoulders for a moment and looking her straight in the eyes. "Don't think you're the only one who's finding this difficult."

"Finding what difficult?" asked Mrs. Grace, coming through the door. She gave her husband a kiss and added, "Hello, dear. Good to see you home early for a change."

"Nothing in particular," Mr. Grace replied, with a last warning look at Josie. "Oh, before I forget, Mary, there were a couple of messages on the answering machine. The Randalls want you to call them back, and someone else I hadn't heard of. Atter—something, I think."

The Randalls! Josie felt her heart leap. Had they called to say they wanted to buy Faith? And what would her mother decide, if they had?

"Thanks. I'll call from in here," her mother said, taking off her coat and going into the study. She closed the door behind her.

"Why don't you and I go into the kitchen, Josie," said her father. "I could do with a willing assistant, and I'm sure Mom doesn't want you hanging on her every word. Come on." And he walked her down the corridor, a gentle hand on her back.

"I know it's not easy for Mom, either," Josie said as they went into the kitchen, "but at least she gets to decide where Faith ends up."

"Well, your opinion counts, too," Mr. Grace said, taking a handful of carrots from the vegetable rack. "You know your mother always listens to what you say. But someone has to make the final decision. And that person should be her. And anyway, she'd never let Faith go to anyone who wasn't going to treat her properly."

"You're right," Josie admitted, rummaging in a drawer for the vegetable peeler. "Maybe it's just the idea of Faith going away from us at all that's so hard to take. But if you'd seen the Hyde-Whites, Dad, you'd understand. They're so rich and stuck-up." She began to peel the carrots. "Still, maybe the Randalls were calling to say they want Faith, and Mom will sell her to them, and then I'll have something else to worry about."

"No, that's one worry you can cross off your list, Josie," said her mother, coming into the kitchen. "The Randalls aren't going up to Scotland after all. Mr. Randall was offered a fantastic deal today by his present company so he'd stay with them, and that's what he's decided to do. They said the only thing they really regretted was that now they wouldn't be able to have Faith."

"Oh," said Josie, pausing with the peeler in midair. "I don't know whether to be disappointed or relieved."

"I know exactly how you feel," said her mother, sitting at the table and running a hand through her hair. "It's great that Faith isn't going up to Scotland, but it's a pity the Randalls can't have her. I'm afraid this leaves the way clear for the Hyde-Whites, Josie."

"What about the other people who left a message?" asked Mr. Grace.

"I couldn't get hold of them," Mrs. Grace replied, "though I'll keep trying. But unless an ideal offer comes along before Friday, I simply can't see a better alternative for Faith than going to Littlehaven Hall. That's all there is to it."

CHAPTER
EIGHT

Josie gave one last look for Anna and Ben as the bus for school approached the stop. They always seemed to leave at the very last minute. The double doors were just swishing shut as she caught a glimpse of two figures running up the road.

"Hang on—they're just coming!" she said to the bus driver.

He sighed, shaking his head. "One day, I won't wait," he said, pressing a button to reopen the doors. "That'll teach them a lesson."

"Sorry! Thanks!" panted Anna as she threw herself up the steps next to Josie and slapped down the money for her fare.

"Ought to get yourself an alarm clock," the

driver said grumpily to Ben as he followed his sister.

"Come on, it's the first time we've been late this week," Ben replied, tearing his ticket out of the machine.

"Well done! It's only Tuesday," the driver called after him as the three of them went down the aisle to their usual seats near the back.

"Well?" Anna said, as soon as she'd got her breath again. "How did it go yesterday, with the Hyde-Whites?"

"Oh, you can imagine," Josie said. "They've got this amazing house, and wonderful stables with a groom and everything. They're happy to have Faith, but they don't want to be bothered with us coming to visit her. We're not on their level—they made that very clear."

"So did you decide anything?" Ben asked. "You've still got that other family interested, haven't you? The ones who are going up to Scotland?"

"No, that's the other thing," Josie said. "They called yesterday to say that they're not moving after all, so they won't be able to buy Faith. At the moment, it's the Hyde-Whites or nothing—apart from some people Mom hasn't been able to speak to who left a message on the machine. Harriet just has to give her gracious approval, and then Faith will be all theirs. She's coming to check her out on Friday evening."

"You *can't* let Faith go to the Hyde-Whites," Anna said. "It would be all wrong! How can your mother even consider it?"

"Because they've got stables and a groom, and plenty of land, and they know all about horses," Josie said. "Anyway, there doesn't seem to be any other option at the moment. What else can we do?"

"I've been thinking this over," Anna said, as the bus rumbled on its way through the winding country roads. "Just tell me—do you agree, the main thing is to get the Hyde-Whites out of the picture?"

"I'm not sure," Josie said doubtfully. Then she thought back to the huge cold house, and the unsmiling groom, and the sharp woman on her dressage horse, and came to a decision. "Yes!" she said firmly. "You're right. I don't want Faith to go with the Hyde-Whites!"

"Good," Anna said. "Then you leave it to Ben and me. It might be better if you didn't know too much about the plan so that you won't get into trouble with your mother. She might not be so hard on us. Besides, you're so hopeless at keeping secrets, you'd be bound to give the plan away."

"What plan is this?" Ben asked. "Is it going to end up with us both getting into trouble, as usual?"

"Look, Ben, do you want to help Josie or not?" Anna demanded. "If you don't then, fine—leave it up to me. But I've thought of something that might do the trick, and it'll be easier if you're in on it too. If it works, no one needs to know we were involved at all."

"And what if it doesn't work?" Ben asked, giving his sister a sharp look. "Your amazing schemes have been known to fail in the past."

"Yes," Josie chimed in. "Remember the catching-a-bus-on-the-cross-country-run idea, and the sneaking-out-of-school-to-buy-an-ice-cream one? They weren't huge successes, were they?"

"Well, at least we'll know we've tried, rather than just sitting here doing nothing," Anna said firmly, rooting among the exercise books in her bag. "Anyway, this plan's foolproof. Now, I suppose I'd better look at those history dates I should have learned last night. Ben, I'll fill you in later about what we're going to do."

Ben looked at Josie and she raised her eyebrows at him. What on earth was Anna dreaming up?

Over the next few days, no matter how hard she tried, Josie couldn't get Anna or Ben to spill any information about their plan. So she tried to put the Hyde-Whites' visit out of her mind and spent as much time with Faith as she could. The days came and went, filled with schoolwork and stable chores and riding. Now that the evenings were getting lighter, she had more time to take Faith out after school, and they went for a couple of long rides through the fields. It was soothing to groom her, too, and Josie took pride in making sure Faith's bay coat was shining and her hooves were oiled.

"That horse looks immaculate," her mother smiled, coming into the stable early on Friday morning. "They're not coming until this evening, you know." It was the first time she'd spoken about the Hyde-Whites since their visit to Littlehaven Hall.

"Mom, do we really not have a choice?" Josie

asked, giving Faith a firm stroke with the braided hay wisp, to tone up her muscles.

"There just isn't anyone else on the scene that can match their setup," her mother said decisively. "I did manage to get a hold of the Atterburys—the people who left a phone message—but I had to tell them we had another offer on the table."

"And who are the Atterburys?" Josie asked. "Are they local? Do you know them?"

"Yes and no," her mother replied, taking a body brush and starting to work on Faith's tail. "They moved to Littlehaven a little while ago, but I've never met them. It's quite a sad story, actually. Their daughter, Jill, had her own horse, but she was involved in a car accident last year. She dislocated and fractured her hip very badly, and the doctors told her it would be a long time before she could ride again—if ever."

"Oh, how awful!" Josie exclaimed, letting the wisp fall to the ground.

"I know," said her mother, nodding. "Just imagine that. It puts our problems into perspective, doesn't it? Anyway, they sold her horse and all the tack, but apparently Jill's been beside herself without him. They thought getting an older horse that she could look after, even if she couldn't ride it, might make things a bit easier."

"Well, couldn't we let *them* have Faith?" Josie asked eagerly. "Doesn't that sound like a good idea?"

"It sounds more like you're clutching at straws to me," her mother replied. "I'm really not sure it would be so good from Faith's point of view. They don't have any other horses, for one thing, and she'd hate to be on her own after living here. And she's going to need *some* exercising, too." She put down the brush and, giving Faith a farewell pat, took Josie's arm. "Now come on—time for breakfast, or you'll miss the bus."

The day flew by. Even French class, which was usually an endurance test for Josie, didn't seem to last as long as she'd have liked. Before she knew it, Anna was waving good-bye to her at the bus stop.

"See you later—we'll come by about six," she said. "We'll need a little bit of time alone with Faith and Harriet, but that shouldn't be too difficult to manage. Whatever happens, don't look surprised, okay? Just go with the flow."

Josie made one final appeal. "Ben, are you sure you know what you're doing?" she asked. "No one's going to get hurt, are they?"

"Well, not exactly," he replied with a smile. "Look, this might be a crazy idea, but I think it's worth a try—Anna's convinced me. Just trust us!"

"Why do you both have to be so secretive?" Josie grumbled, a couple of hours later, as she, Anna, and Ben hung around the yard waiting for the Hyde-Whites to arrive. They still wouldn't give her any clues about what they were planning, and it was driving her crazy. "I just wish you'd tell me what you've got in mind!" she said, for the twentieth time.

"Believe me," Anna said, "the less you know, the better."

"I know, why don't we go and clean some tack?" Ben suggested. "That'll help pass the time, if there's nothing else we can be doing."

They were sitting quietly working away in the tack room when the Hyde-Whites' car pulled up.

"Are you up to something?" Mrs. Grace asked, stopping for a moment as she walked past the open tack-room door on her way to greet them. "You don't usually go in there unless I've bribed you with a ride first."

"Come on, you guys," Anna said, jumping to her feet. "Let's go and make friends with Harriet." Mrs. Grace looked even more suspicious as the three of them trooped out after her.

Mr. Hyde-White and his daughter were just getting out of the car. Harriet was exactly as Josie had remembered: thick strawberry-blond hair and a tanned, thin face which, she now realized, was the image of her mother's. She was wearing a spotless pale-blue cotton sweater and a pair of jodhpurs that looked brand new.

"Hello, Harriet," Josie said, feeling as though she ought to make an effort.

"Yes, hi," said Anna, flashing her a big smile. "It's great to see you again."

Looking slightly surprised, Harriet gave them a cool nod in return.

"We meet again," said Mr. Hyde-White. "We are seeing a lot of each other, aren't we?" And he gave his short, barking laugh.

"Faith's waiting for you in the stall," Mrs. Grace said. She led the way over, with the Hyde-Whites following behind and Ben, Josie, and Anna bringing up the rear. Harriet obviously didn't want to talk to them, and stuck very close to her father's side.

Faith was standing with her head over the stable door, watching them approach. Hope looked the visitors over, too, but Charity stayed somewhere in the depths of her stable. Mrs. Grace brought Faith out into the sunshine, and Josie watched as Harriet examined her closely from head to foot. There was a slightly awkward atmosphere, as though no one knew quite what to say. Mrs. Grace seemed to sense it too, and after a while she handed the lead rope to Ben, who happened to be standing next to her, and said, "Why don't you saddle Faith up so Harriet can have a ride on her? I'll take Mr. Hyde-White to the office for a chat while you spend some time on your own."

"Good idea," Mr. Hyde-White said. "We can talk business while the younger generation talks horses, right? See you later, Hatty."

Harriet looked a little alarmed at being left on her own, but Anna immediately went into her most charming mode. "Josie's told us all about your wonderful stables," she said, with a warm smile. "Faith would be so lucky to have a home with you."

"Well, I'm sure she's had enough of beginners thumping about on her like sacks of potatoes," Harriet replied, with a thin smile. "She'll think she's died and gone to heaven if she comes to us."

Anna continued chatting in such an easy, friendly way that anyone would have thought she wanted to be Harriet's best friend. She flattered her so cleverly that frosty Harriet began to thaw in spite of herself. Then, very subtly, she led the conversation so that it left Josie out in the cold. It soon began to sound as though Anna had never liked Josie much in the first place, and only came to the stables because she wanted a chance to ride. Harriet sensed what was happening and was quite happy to add her own snide remarks. Soon she and Anna were clearly on one side of the fence with Josie on the other. No one bothered much about Ben, who ended up getting Faith's tack and saddling her up while the three girls talked.

Although she could tell Anna was up to something, Josie couldn't help feeling a little bit hurt by the way she was being treated.

"Why don't you get those photos of you and Faith when you were a little girl?" Anna said to her eventually. "I'm sure Harriet would like to see them, and I want to talk to her without you hanging around all the time like our shadow. Go on, we'll see you later. Ben's going to take Faith to the arena for us."

"Take as long as you like—we won't mind," added Harriet with a sneer. Picking on somebody else seemed to have brought her to life; there was a glint in her eye and she looked like she was really enjoying herself.

"Okay," said Josie, beginning to understand what Anna was working toward. She'd said she needed some time on her own with Harriet, and shutting Josie out was one way to get it. "I won't be too long," she added, but Anna had already taken Harriet's arm, and was whispering into her ear.

Josie walked off to the house, so that the next stage of the mysterious plan—whatever it was—could be put into effect. Up in her room, she lay on the bed and waited.

Five minutes later, everything started happening. Josie heard a sudden shout from Ben and a neigh from Faith. Rushing out of her room, she went to the landing window and looked down at the yard.

Faith was tossing up her head and dancing backward, plainly upset about something. Ben had dropped her reins and was bending over, clutching his arm. Josie saw Anna and Harriet come running up to him from a little way behind, and then all three of them stood clustered together for a moment. Next, Harriet broke away from the group and stormed over to the office, flinging open the door.

Josie had seen enough. She rushed down the stairs and through the front door, then along the path and out into the yard. "What's going on?" she cried, rushing up to Ben and Anna.

"I'm not sure," Anna replied. "Wait and see." She had taken Faith's reins and, giving the horse a gentle pat, talked quietly to calm her down. Faith's ears were back and she was showing the whites of her eyes.

"Are you okay?" Josie asked Ben. "Has something happened to Faith?"

"Oh, I'm fine," he said, still holding his arm. "Faith's just a bit startled, that's all. Sorry, old girl," he added, "but we had to do it. It's for your own good."

"What's for her own good?" Josie asked frantically. "What have you done?"

"Tell you later—they're coming out," Anna hissed. "Stand away from me, Josie!"

Mr. Hyde-White and Harriet came out of the office on the opposite side of the yard, followed by Mrs. Grace. "I don't understand," Josie's mom was saying. "I just can't believe what you're saying. It's completely untrue!"

"You would say that, wouldn't you?" Harriet replied nastily, as she opened the car door.

"It's quite clear you haven't been straight with us," Mr. Hyde-White said angrily, getting into the driver's seat. He wound down the window and continued, "I consider our business here finished. You have behaved in a most underhand way and completely wasted my valuable time. Then again, I never rated your shabby little stables very highly. Should have guessed something like this would happen."

With that, the engine roared into life, and the large shiny car shot out of the yard.

Mrs. Grace looked across to where Ben, Anna, and Josie were standing with Faith. "You three!" she shouted. "I want a word with you!"

"Now who's going to tell me what on earth's going

on?" Mrs. Grace said angrily, staring at Josie and Anna as they stood in front of her desk in the crowded little office. "And where's Ben?"

"He's putting Faith back in her stall," Anna said.

"So who is going to tell me where this ridiculous story about Faith being vicious has come from?" Mrs. Grace demanded.

"What?" said Josie, horrified. "I don't know what you mean!"

"No, I can see you don't," said her mother, looking at her face. "Well, Anna?"

"It was my idea," Anna said. "Josie didn't know anything about it." She took a deep breath. "We felt that it would be awful for Faith to go to the Hyde-Whites—none of us would be able to see her again. So I thought, if we couldn't put *you* off the idea, we'd have to put *them* off her instead."

"Go on," said Mrs. Grace in an icy voice, as Anna seemed to have dried up.

Anna cleared her throat. "Well, I sucked up to Harriet, and then when we were on our own I told her that Faith had this terrible habit of savagely biting other horses, and people as well. And that was why you wanted to sell her."

Josie stared at Anna. She didn't know what to think. Part of her thought it was a brilliant idea, and part of her wanted to laugh at the very thought of Faith biting anyone. The biggest part of all, though, was terrified of how her mother would react, as she sat there with a face like thunder.

"And she believed you just like that?" Mrs. Grace asked. "She even swallowed some story you'd made up about Ben having been bitten?"

"Well, there was a bit more to it than that," Ben said, coming through the door and standing next to his sister. "I'd better show you this." And he rolled up one shirtsleeve and held out his arm.

Josie couldn't stop herself from screaming at the sight. A deep open wound, the edges raw and gaping, stretched its ugly way along Ben's right forearm.

CHAPTER NINE

"Oh, my goodness!" exclaimed Mrs. Grace, clutching the edge of the table in shock.

"Ben!" Josie cried. "What happened to you?" She didn't understand how he could stand there so calmly when he must be in agony.

"Oh, it's all right," he replied. "Watch!" And he began to peel the wound away from his arm with his left hand, leaving smooth brown skin behind.

"It's plastic," Anna explained. "Ben was given this pack of stage makeup for his birthday last year —which is what gave me the whole idea! These wounds are so realistic. We put one of them on his arm at home, under his shirt. When he was leading Faith over to the ring in front of Harriet and me, he kind of jerked her head up and pretended that she'd bitten him. You'd never have guessed it was fake, would you?"

"No, I wouldn't!" Mrs. Grace said, letting out her breath in a rush. "You nearly gave me a heart attack. Still, that's the least of it." She got up from her chair and, folding her arms, stared at Ben and Anna for a moment before speaking.

"Did you think for one second about the consequences of what you were doing?" she said. "Did you not stop to consider where your crazy scheme would leave Faith? That it would take away her chance of going to a good home?"

"But we didn't think it *was* a good home, Mrs. Grace," Anna said. "Harriet's not a kind person, and we didn't think that anybody there would love Faith the way they should. The way we do."

"I know the Hyde-Whites have got all the right facilities, Mom, but they're so unfeeling," Josie added. "Faith needs someone who'll give her lots of affection, you know she does!"

Her mother sighed. "We've had this conversation before," she said. "You're perfectly well aware of what I think. That's partly why I'm so angry," she went on, turning to Anna. "I know you only did what you thought was best to help Josie, but you undermined me completely. You made me look like an idiot—and what's worse, a liar—in front of that man."

"I'm sorry, Mrs. Grace," Anna said, beginning to look ashamed and staring at her shoes. "I didn't really think about that."

"Well, you should have," she replied. "I'm beginning to think none of you understand what's at stake here. We *have* to find somewhere else for Faith to live. We can't keep her, however much we'd all like to—me more than anyone. And what am I supposed to do now?" She looked at the three of them despairingly.

"Call the Atterburys?" Josie suggested hopefully.

"I suppose I'll have to," her mother said. "Though who knows whether they're really interested. In the meantime, Ben and Anna, you are banned from coming here until I give permission. And none of you are *ever* to pull a stunt like that again. Do you understand me? If you really disagree with something, come and talk to me about it. Don't just take the law into your own hands. Okay?"

"Okay," the three of them replied together. Then, with muttered good-byes and sorrys and a quick wave to Josie, Ben and Anna shuffled out of the office.

Mrs. Grace shook her head and looked at Josie. "At least they had the sense to keep you out of this," she said. "That girl! What will she think of next?"

"Sorry, Mom," Josie said. "I'm sure she didn't mean to land you in it."

"Well, she did, whether she meant to or not," Mrs. Grace said, reaching for the phone book. "And she certainly got rid of the Hyde-Whites pretty quickly. I've never seen anyone move so fast! Now, I'm going to call the Atterburys and have a talk with them—in private. This time, you leave things to me."

"Okay, Mom," Josie replied. "Message understood." She ran out of the office, feeling she'd gotten off lightly.

Josie didn't rush through the evening chores. She groomed the horses carefully and turned them out, one by one. Mary Collins was out for a ride on Tubber, and her mother had already taken care of Captain and Connie. By the time Josie had come back into the house, her parents were sitting talking quietly together at the kitchen table over an open bottle of wine. Good! she thought to herself, Mom's probably calmed down by now. She snatched a quick look at her mother's face, just to make sure.

Mrs. Grace noticed her glance. "There's no need to tiptoe around me like I'm going to explode," she said. "I've stopped seething now. You can understand how I felt, though, can't you?"

"*I* certainly can," said Mr. Grace. "I'm not going to go on and on about this, Josie, but remember what I said about things being hard for other people, not just you? Well, I expect you to be helping your mother, not going behind her back."

"To be fair, Rob, I don't think Josie knew much about it," said her mother, putting a hand over her husband's.

"I knew something was going on, but I wasn't sure exactly what," Josie said, pulling up a chair and sitting down at the table. "We were all so certain that Littlehaven Hall wasn't the right place for Faith, Mom, and nothing I said to you seemed to make any difference."

Mrs. Grace took a sip from her glass and stared

at Josie thoughtfully. "I can see that must have been frustrating," she said. "Perhaps we should have spent more time talking it over. I really felt Faith would be well looked after there, that's all. I know the Hyde-Whites aren't particularly friendly, but I thought maybe that wouldn't matter to Faith. I was sure they'd never have mistreated her."

"But how would we have known, Mom?" Josie asked. "They'd never have let us back into their precious home to visit her, would they?"

"No, they wouldn't," Mrs. Grace agreed. She leaned back in her chair and stretched her arms up above her head. "Well, we'll never know now. I don't think Mr. Hyde-White will come back to our shabby little stables in a hurry!"

"Is that what he called them?" Mr. Grace said. "What nerve! Well, if he does come back, I'll set him straight." He waved a napkin in the air. "Teach him a lesson! Littlehaven Hall or no Littlehaven Hall."

"Groom or no groom!" Josie said, smiling. "You go for it, Dad!"

"Dressage horse or no dressage horse!" added Mrs. Grace, getting into the spirit of things. "We'll teach that rascal a lesson!"

Josie gave her mother a hug. "I'm sorry, Mom," she said. "I'm sorry you had to stand there while he talked to you like that."

"Oh, well," said her mother, stroking Josie's auburn hair, "I expect I'll survive. I've heard worse than that before. And while I'm not quite ready to forgive Anna completely for what she's done, things sometimes have a funny habit of working out in the end."

"How do you mean?" Josie asked, drawing back to look at her mother's face.

"Well, I got a hold of the Atterburys," she said, "and they are definitely still interested, though they don't want to get Jill's hopes up at this stage. They'd like to come over on their own early tomorrow morning, and take a look at Faith. *I'll* talk to them and *you* can hover around in the background. Understood? This time, we'll play everything by the book."

"Okay, Mom," Josie said, just happy that everything was back to normal. "Whatever you say."

"Josie? Is that you?" hissed an urgent voice on the other end of the phone, the next afternoon.

"Anna?" Josie replied. "Yes, it's me—Mom's out teaching a lesson, luckily for you. How are you guys? Does your mom know about everything?"

"Yes, we told her," Anna said. "We thought it would come out sooner or later. She's made us write letters of apology and she's going to bring them by tonight and take your mom out. Don't say anything, though—it's meant to be a surprise. How is she? Still in a bad mood?"

"She's getting over it," Josie replied. "You're crazy, Anna, you know that? How on earth did you think you'd get away with that?"

"I never thought Harriet would make such a fuss," Anna said. "I thought they'd just leave and then she'd say something to her dad when they were on their own. Oh, I don't know—I suppose I didn't really think that part of it through. Still, you've got to admit the plan worked. We got rid of the Hyde-Whites, didn't we?"

"*You* certainly did," Josie said. "Look, I can't talk too long. The lesson's nearly over, and then Mom and I are going to see some other people who might buy Faith."

"Who are they?" Anna asked. "Are they nice?

Do they love horses? Do you know where they live?"

"The Atterburys live in Littlehaven," Josie said, "and I don't know what they're like. After your performance yesterday I decided to keep out of the way when they came over this morning. Mom spoke to them and she hasn't told me anything yet. They came and looked at Faith without Jill, their daughter. She's had this accident and she can't ride."

"Well then, why does she want a horse?" Anna asked. "Is she crazy or something?"

"Look, I'll explain it later," Josie said. "There really isn't time to go into everything now. We can talk about it on Monday. Oh, and by the way, Anna—thanks. Thanks for everything you did, and Ben, too. Just don't do it again. Okay?"

"Charming," Anna retorted. "And there was me thinking we'd done you a huge favor."

"You did, you did!" Josie replied. "I owe you one. It was a bit dramatic, that's all. Hang on, I can hear Mom calling. Got to go. See you soon!"

She put down the receiver and hurried out of the house. The lesson was over and Mrs. Grace was helping a pupil dismount from Hope.

"Can you help Sally, please?" she called when she saw Josie. "If you could take Faith from her, I'll follow you up to the stalls with Hope, and then we can go. Okay?"

"You're selling Faith, aren't you?" Sally asked, taking her feet out of the stirrups, then swinging her leg over Faith's back and slithering to the ground. "Have you found someone to buy her yet?"

"Not yet," Josie replied, looping the reins over Faith's head and handing them back to Sally so she could hold her while the saddle was heaved off. "Still, I'm sure it won't take us too long. Mom and I are going to look at another place in a minute. Don't you worry, old girl," she added, giving Faith a pat before she ran up the stirrup straps and unbuckled the girth. "We'll come up with the perfect home, just you wait and see."

But she couldn't help listening to a little voice that kept nagging her in the back of her mind. *What if nothing turns up?* it said. *What will we do then? Was turning the Hyde-Whites away a big mistake after all?*

"So," Josie said to her mother as she fastened her

seat belt twenty minutes later, "tell me what you think about the Atterburys. I finally tried to keep out of the way this morning, didn't I?"

Josie had brought Faith in from the field first thing and given her a thorough grooming so she looked her best. When the Atterburys arrived, she had made herself busy catching Hope and Charity. Apart from a quick hello, she hadn't talked to them at all.

"Yes, you did," her mother smiled, as she reversed their car out of the yard. "You were very discreet. Well, I liked them. They've had such a worrying time with Jill—it must have been awful! She was out for the day with a friend and some lunatic drove straight into the car they were in. Anyway, they sold her horse on the doctor's advice."

"Poor Jill," Josie said, shaking her head. "I can't imagine how I'd cope with the prospect of not being able to ride."

Her mother nodded. "Apparently Jill misses the horse desperately," she said. "Not just for riding, but all the time she spent grooming and feeding, even mucking out! Just having one around the place again would mean such a lot to her."

"And did her parents like Faith?" Josie asked.

"What do you think?" Mrs. Grace replied. "Everybody likes her, that's the trouble! They thought she was wonderful—that's why they wanted us to come over as soon as possible to see their place and talk it over."

"So is this it, Mom?" Josie asked, as they approached the outskirts of Littlehaven. "Do you think they're the right family for Faith?"

"I'm not sure," Mrs. Grace said thoughtfully. "There are a few things to consider. I don't know whether Faith's ready to retire completely, for one thing. She'll need some exercise for a while. And she might get lonely, all on her own. I think we must be really careful not to get Jill's hopes up, just in case it doesn't work out."

Ten minutes later, they were pulling up outside a modern detached house near the edge of town. Josie caught sight of a face at the window, which instantly vanished. Seconds later, the front door opened and Mrs. Atterbury was smiling at them, her arm around the shoulder of a thin, pale girl with shoulder-length brown hair. "Jill's been waiting for you to arrive all afternoon," she said, as Mrs. Grace and Josie got out of the car. "I thought she was going to burn a hole looking through that window!"

"Hi, Jill," Josie said as she walked up the path. "I'm Josie. Hello, Mrs. Atterbury."

"Thanks for coming," Jill said shyly, standing back. She was probably about ten or eleven, Josie thought, with a serious face and big dark eyes that seemed to take everything in.

They all stood around for a little while in the hall, and then Mrs. Atterbury said to her daughter, "Why don't you take Josie to your room, Jill? You could show her your pictures of Marmalade."

"Okay. It's just down here," Jill said to Josie, pointing along the path.

"Do you need this?" Mrs. Atterbury said, holding out a walking stick that was propped against the wall.

Jill shook her head. "I can manage," she said abruptly.

Josie followed her down the path, trying not to take any notice of Jill dragging one leg along awkwardly as she walked. "I had crutches for three months," Jill said, glancing back. "I'm trying to do without anything now so that my leg will get stronger."

"It must be a real pain," Josie commented, wishing she could think of something more original to say.

"Certainly is," Jill replied. "But it's a great excuse for getting out of gym."

They both laughed, for just a little bit longer than the joke was worth. Josie felt a huge sense of relief that the ice was broken. Jill had obviously gotten used to making people feel comfortable about what had happened to her.

"This is my room," she said, opening the door. "It used to be the study, but Mom and Dad fixed it up as a bedroom for me so I didn't have to keep climbing the stairs."

"It looks great!" Josie said, staring around at the hundreds of horse and pony pictures covering every inch of the walls. "I've never seen so many posters. I've got that one, too—the gray galloping along the beach. He's beautiful, isn't he?"

"That's my favorite," Jill said. "I lie in bed sometimes looking at it and imagining I'm on his back, riding off into the sunset."

"Does that make you feel worse?" Josie asked sympathetically, sitting down on a chair by the desk.

Although she'd only just met Jill, she felt as though she could talk to her about anything.

"Not really," Jill replied. "I know I'm going to be riding again some day. I've made my mind up that I will." She reached up for a photo album on the bookshelf and flipped open the pages. "Look, this is me on Marmalade," she said, showing Josie some pictures of herself sitting proudly on a beautifully turned-out light bay horse.

"Oh, he's handsome!" Josie exclaimed, putting the album down on the desktop to look more closely at the photograph. "Do you have any other photos of him?"

"Loads," Jill said, coming to stand behind her and turning over the pages in the album. "See, there we are jumping—we'd just started together. This is us in the pole bending race. We came second, you know. I've got the rosette up on my bulletin board. Oh, I do miss him," she added with a sigh, staring out of the window. "I wish we hadn't sold him so quickly. It's just not the same without a horse around."

"I can imagine," Josie said, thinking of all the time she spent looking after their three. She followed Jill's gaze and saw her mother with Mrs. Atterbury at the end of the yard, looking out over the field that lay beyond. "Is that your field?" she said. "Where you kept Marmalade?"

"That's right," Jill said. "You'd never have thought there was all this land here, would you? It's perfect for horses—there's a little stream at the bottom, and a shelter too." She turned to Josie with an eager expression. "Now, come on—tell me all about Faith. From what Mom and Dad have said, she sounds perfect."

She grasped the arm of Josie's chair and used it to lower herself awkwardly into a sitting position on the edge of the bed, her leg stuck out straight in front of her. "Where did she come from? What does she like doing? I want to know everything!" she demanded.

Josie wasn't quite sure what to say. She remembered what her mother had told her about not raising Jill's hopes. She liked Jill a lot, but would she really be able to cope with another horse just yet? And would Faith be happy, all by herself in that big field?

"Look, Jill," she began, "before I start boring you

to death, maybe there are a few things we ought to talk about. We think Faith's going to need riding for a while. And she's used to being with other animals—I just don't know if she'd be happy on her own the whole time. . . ."

Josie's voice trailed away, as she tried to think of a tactful way of saying what was on her mind. Then she decided just to be honest about it. "Look, Jill, I'd love you to have Faith—more than anyone else we've seen so far—but do you really think this is the right place for her?"

CHAPTER
TEN

"Oh, you don't need to worry about any of that," Jill said, waving her hand. "It's all arranged! Faith wouldn't be on her own, for one thing. And the riding's taken care of, too."

"What do you mean?" Josie asked, looking at her curiously. Had Jill understood what she was trying to say?

Jill leaned forward from her seat on the bed. "Listen, as soon as Mom and Dad told me about your horse, we called my friend Bev. She's been renting the field from us for her gelding, Midnight. He's a big horse, but he's gentle as a lamb—Faith would just love him. Bev's already taken him out for a ride this afternoon, or you could meet him and you'd see what I mean. Anyway, there's plenty of room for both of them in the field and the shelter, too! Bev thinks he's lonely at the moment, so she'd like him to have some company."

Josie felt a tingle begin to creep its way up her spine. There was something about the way everything was falling into place that made her feel this new home was meant to be. "That sounds great!" she said. "Provided they get along, of course."

"Midnight gets along with everyone," Jill said. "He's a big soppy marshmallow. Plus, Bev and her sister would love to take Faith out sometimes—if you agree, that is. They're horse crazy and they've been riding for years, so they'd take care of her."

"Oh, Jill, you really have thought it all through," said Josie, delighted. "I think that sounds perfect! You'd look after Faith—she'd be your horse, but other people would exercise her sometimes for you."

"There is someone else I probably ought to let ride her," Jill said seriously.

"Oh? Who?" Josie asked, wondering what was coming.

"You, of course!" Jill said, laughing at her bewildered expression. "You could come and take

Faith out whenever you felt like it. I know you'll be moving out of the stables, but you probably won't end up that far away from us."

"Jill, that would be wonderful!" Josie said, unable to stop the tears coming to her eyes. "You don't know how much that would mean to me."

"Well, maybe we shouldn't get carried away," Jill said, embarrassed. "Maybe we should go and see what our mothers have decided first."

"I just want to say one thing," Josie said, blowing her nose on a scrap of tissue she found in her pocket. "If you do take Faith, she'll be your horse, not ours anymore. I don't want you to feel that I'd be hanging around all the time. If Mom decides that this is the right place for her too, then I couldn't be happier handing her over to you."

"If you go on like this I'll have to throw that snotty tissue at you," said Jill. "Come on, give me a hand and let's go down to the field. You can tell me all about Faith on the way."

Josie and her mother hardly said a word on the way back to Grace's Stables. It was obvious to them both that since they couldn't keep Faith anymore, the next-best home she could possibly find was with the Atterburys. When Josie had gone out into the yard with Jill, she had known from her mother's face that she had made up her mind.

"We'd better not keep you in suspense any longer," Mrs. Grace had said, smiling at Jill's anxious expression. "Come and have a look at Faith tomorrow. If you like her as much as your parents did—and if Josie agrees—she's yours."

"I've already decided that Faith would love it here," Josie said, beaming at her mom.

"And you're bound to love Faith, Jill," Mrs. Atterbury said. "She's gorgeous—just wait till you see her."

"Oh, I *can't* wait!" Jill cried, throwing her arms around her mother and nearly falling over in excitement. "I'll take such good care of her, Josie, I promise you! And you must come and see her whenever you want. Thank you, Mom! Thank you, everybody!"

They arranged for Jill to come over the next evening, after lessons were over but before the Graces' big Sunday supper. Then Josie and her mother started out on the drive home, both obviously feeling rather quiet and sad. This is it, Josie thought to herself. Faith is really leaving. Even if they had found a wonderful home for her, it was somebody else's and not theirs.

"All right, sweetie?" asked Mrs. Grace.

Josie nodded, feeling too choked up to speak.

"It's so strange, to think of Faith going away," her mother said. "But I just keep remembering the way Jill looked, when she realized she might be able to have her. She's had to give up so much. She deserves some happiness now, don't you think?"

Josie cleared her throat. "Yes, she does," she said. "She's going to love Faith and look after her, and Faith will love her back. I know this is for the best, Mom—it's just a bit hard, that's all."

"I know," said her mother. "Believe me, I feel it too."

It was quiet in the yard by the time they got back. Basil must have been inside the house, and the birds were all safely shut up in their henhouse for the evening.

"Oh, Lynne's here!" said Mrs. Grace, spotting her friend's blue van in the yard. "Great! I could use some cheering up. She'd better not have brought Ben and Anna, though."

"No, I don't think she has," Josie said. "See you later, Mom. I'll take care of the horses."

"Okay," said her mother. "Don't stay out here moping, though, will you?"

Josie shook her head and walked over to the stalls. Faith was dozing quietly with her lower lip drooping and her long mane falling over her eyes. Josie walked up and rested her head against the horse's smooth, steady neck. "Oh, Faith," she said, her tears beginning to fall. "What are we going to do without you?"

Faith nuzzled Josie's hair gently. Josie looked up into her big brown eyes that had such a wise, intelligent look about them. She wiped her nose with the back of her hand. She thought about Jill, sitting in her room with all the posters and not knowing whether she'd ever be able to ride again. She must have been one of the bravest people Josie had ever met.

"You're going to have a new home and a new owner, Faith," she said. "But I know you'll love her—she's just as special as you are. I think you're going to be really happy together."

Sunday passed in a blur. The Graces tried to have

their normal weekend routine, but Josie could only think about what would happen that evening. She knew her parents were just waiting for the time to pass, too.

"Oh, thank goodness that's over," Mrs. Grace said as she waved good-bye to her last pupil. "It seems to have been such hard work today!"

Josie looked at her watch yet again. Half past four. One hour to go, and then the Atterburys would be here.

Faith hadn't been ridden since the morning, and was looking out of her stall. "You've got no idea what's going to happen, have you?" Josie whispered, stopping to give her a quick stroke as she passed by with Charity. "Well, don't you worry—everything'll work out just fine." She was trying to be brave, but she couldn't stop the butterflies from dancing around in her stomach.

At five, Josie was hanging around the kitchen, getting in her father's way, when she heard a knock on the front door. Mrs. Grace came out of the study to open it, and moments later, Josie heard familiar voices.

"Visitors for you!" her mother announced, as she

came through the kitchen door with Ben and Anna. "Thought you might like some moral support."

"Oh, great, Mom!" said Josie with a broad smile for her friends. "I feel better already."

"Hi, Josie! We've been forgiven," said Anna, coming to stand next to her. "Your mom told ours last night we're allowed back, so we thought we'd surprise you."

"I really appreciated those letters you both wrote," said Mrs. Grace. "And after all, if it hadn't been for you, Faith would probably have ended up with the Hyde-Whites. Not that I'm saying you were right to do what you did," she added hastily.

"It'll never happen again, I promise," Ben said seriously. "Mom made me throw the makeup away."

"Oh, what a shame," said Mr. Grace. "I was thinking of borrowing it."

"Just you try!" said his wife, but at that moment there was another loud knock on the front door. Everyone fell silent and looked at each other. "They're early," Mrs. Grace said, as she went back down the hall.

"I'm sorry, we just couldn't wait any longer," said Mr. Atterbury as he came into the kitchen with his wife and daughter. There was a flurry of smiling and nodding and handshaking as Ben, Anna, and Mr. Grace were introduced. Then, after some halfhearted conversation, Mrs. Grace said, "Well, what are we waiting for? Faith's all ready to meet you, Jill. Why don't you go with Josie and Anna and Ben? We'll join you later."

The four of them walked slowly down the path and across the yard. Why am I so nervous? Josie thought to herself. She looked at Jill's intent, white face and realized she was feeling exactly the same. Linking an arm through hers, she said, "Don't worry—I'm sure this is going to work out."

Jill gave her a smile in return, then tightened her grip as she caught her first glimpse of Faith, looking out of the stall. She stopped and stared for a moment in silence. Faith gave a neigh and shook her mane, as though she was calling. Jill dropped Josie's arm and began to walk as quickly as she could toward the bay horse.

Anna started to go with her, but Josie shook her head. "Let her go alone," she said quietly.

They watched together as Jill went over to where Faith was standing, waiting. She held out her hand, then stroked Faith's white stripe, patted her neck, and tickled her nose. Talking gently all the time, she reached into her pocket and brought out a packet of peppermints. Soon Faith was crunching happily, tossing her head up and down so that her mane shook. Suddenly, she lowered her head and, very gently, nuzzled Jill's forehead with her lips.

"Oh, look!" said Josie delightedly. "She's giving her a kiss! She usually only does that to me and Mom!"

In return, Jill threw her arms around Faith's neck and gave her a huge hug. For a second, she stayed with her face buried in Faith's mane, not moving. Josie felt the tears come to her eyes. Anna grabbed her hand and gave it a squeeze as they looked on silently.

Then Jill turned back to them, grinning from ear to ear. "She's perfect!" she cried. "I love her already. Oh, thank you, Josie!"

After that, it was only a question of working out the arrangements after everyone had gathered together around Faith's stall. It was decided that Mrs. Grace would take Faith over to the Atterburys in the trailer the next day, with her tack and anything else that she might need. "No sense in putting it off, once the decision has been made," Mrs. Grace said.

Jill smiled gratefully. "That would be wonderful," she said. "I just can't wait for Faith to come." Then she gave Josie an anxious look. "If you're sure that'll give you enough time to say your good-byes."

Josie nodded. "Faith and I talked already," she said. "I've told her all about you. Besides, it's not good-bye forever, is it? More like 'see you later.' I'm sure we'll be seeing each other again soon."

"Come on," suggested Anna. "Why don't we go and turn Faith out in the field. She's had enough excitement for one day. Do you want to take her, Jill?"

Jill clipped the lead rein to Faith's bridle and brought her proudly out of the stall. Aware of everyone's watching eyes, she started to make her way rather nervously over toward the field. Faith stayed close by her shoulder, walking slowly and quietly as though she realized she should match her pace to Jill's.

"They look good together, don't you think?" murmured Mrs. Grace, putting a comforting arm around Josie's shoulders.

And, smiling through her tears, Josie had to agree that they did. "Perfect!" she said.

THE HORSESHOE TRILOGIES

Enter
The Horseshoe Trilogies Sweepstakes for a chance to win FREE horseback riding lessons!

NO PURCHASE OR PAYMENT NECESSARY TO ENTER OR WIN, NOR WILL A PURCHASE IMPROVE THE CHANCES OF WINNING.

THE HORSESHOE TRILOGIES SWEEPSTAKES OFFICIAL RULES

1. SPONSOR: Volo Books, an imprint of Disney Children's Book Group, LLC, 114 Fifth Avenue, Room 1426, New York, NY 10011.

2. ENTRY: Hand print your full name, address, daytime phone number (with area code) and birth date, on the official entry form located below, or on a 3" x 5" card, and mail it inside a postage prepaid business size (#10) envelope, to: The Horseshoe Trilogies Sweepstakes, c/o Volo Books, 114 Fifth Avenue, Room 1426, New York, NY 10011.

3. LIMITATIONS: Each entry must be postmarked by 10/01/02, and received by 10/10/02. Only one entry per person/household/family. Open only to persons not older than 16 upon entering who are legal residents of the 50 states or District of Columbia ("Territory") and not employees of Sponsor; its parent, subsidiary or affiliated companies; the advertising, promotional or fulfillment agencies of any of them; (individually and collectively, "Entities") nor members of their immediate families or same households. The Entities are not responsible for entries from persons residing outside the Territory; printing errors; inaccurate, forged, incomplete, stolen, lost, illegible, mutilated, tampered with, postage-due, misdirected, delayed or late entries; each of which will be disqualified. Void where prohibited or restricted by law and subject to all federal, state and local laws and regulations.

4. PRIZE: One (1) GRAND PRIZE: A series of $1,000 worth of horseback riding lessons (approximate retail value: $1,000). The lessons will be offered at such location near to winner's residence as solely determined by Sponsor. All expenses not specifically mentioned herein, including but not limited to the cost of transportation from winner's residence to the location of the rendition of the lessons, are not included and are solely the winner's responsibility. Prize is not redeemable for cash or transferable, except to a surviving spouse residing in the same household. No substitution allowed except, at Sponsor's sole discretion, a prize of equal or greater value may be substituted. The prize will be awarded.

5. PROCEDURES: Sweepstakes begins 6/02/02, and ends 10/01/02. On or about 10/15/02, in a random drawing, under the supervision of the Sponsor whose decisions are final, winner will be selected from all eligible entries received. Odds of winning depend on the number of eligible entries received.

6. WINNER: Will be notified by U.S. Mail on or about 10/17/02. All responsibilities of a minor will be assumed by parent/legal guardian. Disqualification and the selection of an alternate winner will result from any of the following: (1) failure of a potential winner to execute and return an Affidavit of Eligibility/Liability/Publicity, Release within fourteen (14) days from the date of notification; (2) the return of a notification or prize as undeliverable; or (3) any other non-compliance with Official Rules ("Rules"). All taxes are solely the winner's responsibility. For name of winner (after 10/15/02) and/or Rules (before 10/10/02) send a self-addressed, stamped #10 envelope to: The Horseshoe Trilogies Sweepstakes Winner/Rules (designate which), c/o Volo Books, 114 Fifth Avenue, Room 1426, New York, NY 10011.

7. RESERVATIONS: Each entrant by entering this sweepstakes agrees that: (1) he or she will abide by and be bound by the Rules and the judge's decisions; (2) only complete entry forms are eligible; (3) the entry becomes solely the property of the Sponsor and will not be returned; (4) none of the Entities, nor any of their officers, directors, employees, agents or representatives are responsible for claims, injuries, losses, or damages of any kind resulting from sweepstakes participation; the awarding, acceptance, use or misuse of the prize; or participation in any prize related activity; (5) the prize is awarded WITHOUT WARRANTY OF ANY KIND, express or implied; (6) winner's acceptance of the prize constitutes the grant of an unconditional right to use winner's name, address (city and state only), voice, likeness, photograph, biographical and prize information and/or statements about the promotion for any publicity, advertising and promotional purposes without additional compensation, except where prohibited by law; (7) any portion of the prize not accepted by the winner will be

To enter, simply fill out the information below and send in your entry today to:
The Horseshoe Trilogies Sweepstakes, c/o Volo Books,
114 Fifth Avenue, Room 1426, New York, NY 10011

YES! Enter me in The Horseshoe Trilogies Sweepstakes!

Name

Birth date

Address

City

State

Zip